MISSING

No Jurisdiction

RUTH DUCHARME

Missing is the third book in the ever evolving Roland P.D. series.
Killing Frank Barnes
Three Days Gone
Missing

If you would like to receive updates on upcoming releases, you can follow Ruth on Amazon, Facebook, Instagram or Goodreads. You can also subscribe to her newsletter or check out her website at ruthducharme.com
Honest reviews are always coveted!

Chapter One

Harmony, Montana
1991

"Jason! C'mon, lets go!" Marc whispered at the window.

"Geez dude, your gonna wake my mom and then she's gonna kill us both!" I whispered back.

"I guess you'd better get your butt out here then!"

I grunted as I jumped out the window of my first floor bedroom. It was only a few feet from my windowsill to my mother's flowerbed and I cringed as I crushed a few of her favorite daisies. She would kill me if she saw that.

I am grounded and sneaking out was a dumb thing to do but Marc had insisted. He said we were only fourteen once and rules were made to be broken. Marc is also an incorrigible delinquent.

Once I scrambled out from amongst my mom's daisies I grabbed my bike off the front lawn and Marc and I rode down the dark street towards the quarry.

The sky was full of stars and as we rode I couldn't help but look up in admiration and awe. Montana; they don't call it Big Sky country for nothing. It was dark out tonight and even though there were zero streetlights, we didn't need them to navigate this path we knew by heart.

Marc and I live in the small town of Harmony: population 6,000. I was born in Harmony and I never wanted to leave.

I loved living in a small town. Everyone knew each other, everyone helped each other and there were no surprises. I'd read about big cities and all that happened there. Big cities have drugs, murders, serial killers and all kinds of weirdo's. Not in Harmony. The most unsettling things to happen here were maybe a few car burglaries from transients making their way through town or maybe some kids spray painting. The biggest town drama's consisted of kids smoking out behind the high school...yuck...or a girl getting pregnant by her boyfriend. Double Yuck.

The big city had guns and violence. Don't get me wrong, most everyone in Harmony owned and carried a gun, but here, hunting for one's dinner was the norm and self-protection against bears or snakes took precedents. In my fourteen years I had never heard of anyone in Harmony shooting another person! We all went to church on Sundays and our neighbors looked out for us. Harmony was a safe, comfy place to grow up and all my friends and family were here. I loved Harmony and I was going to live here till the day I died.

Marc doesn't share my love for Harmony. He is forever talking about leaving and even though he's my best friend, I think he's nuts. He's an adventurer by heart and he has wild fantasies about leaving town on a train like a darn hobo. Did I tell you he was nuts?

My mom says Marc and I were born in the same hospital on the same day and that's why we are two peas in a pod. I don't know if that is true but Marc is definitely like a brother to me. I don't know what Marc's mom would say about us being two peas in a pod. I've never met Marc's mom. He hasn't either. She died the day he was born.

When Marc was born his mom and dad brought him home and there were some kind of complications. Marc's mom died right there in bed holding him. Marc doesn't really talk about that but I think it bothers him a lot.

I hated that story. It made me sad. I don't know what I'd do without my mom. But maybe if you never had one you can't miss what you never had? Anyway, It was just Marc and his dad and it always had been. His dad had never remarried. I didn't really like Marc's dad. Marc didn't like him either. For some reason his dad was grouchy all the time. And he drank too much. Mom said it's because he's sad and never got over his wife dying but I don't care. Just because something bad happens to you doesn't mean you get to take it out on everyone else. And you especially shouldn't take it out on your only kid. Mom said we had to be kind to Marc's dad and take special care of Marc. I just knew that Marc had always been my friend and he always would be.

Marc spent most of his free time at our house and we were forever getting into trouble together. Which is exactly why I was grounded right now. If my mom could've gotten away with grounding Marc too she would've. My mom and dad loved him almost as much as they loved me.

So while I was supposed to be home in bed reading or something, Marc and I had decided to go for a night swim at the quarry. Marc was ahead of me but turned to look back over his shoulder, "Hurry up Jason!! Last one there is a rotten egg."

DID I mention he was bossy?

Chapter Two

IT ONLY TOOK US ABOUT FIFTEEN MINUTES TO RIDE TO THE TREE line that surrounded the quarry. This place was the biggest swimming hole in the valley and everyone came here to jump, everyone except me that is. I never jumped.

The jump was only about 20 feet but I'd never been brave enough to do it. I usually just find my way to the water line and swim while the other kids, braver than me, practice their swan dives and cannonballs. And no, I don't feel like I'm missing out.

Every time we come to swim the other kids tease me and try to shame me into jumping. I always find a way to get out of it but today had been the last straw and I had gotten into a fistfight over it. Actually, I wouldn't call it a fight. Johnny Thompson had punched me and then Marc had wiped the forest floor with him.

I hated fighting. I was always afraid I'd hurt someone or someone would hurt me. JT had managed to bloody my nose and when he egged me into fighting back I just couldn't do it. Even Marc had yelled for me to get up and hit him back but I was too scared. So when JT took another run at me, Marc whooped him good. Marc wasn't afraid of anything ever.

That fight was why I was grounded and also why I had let Marc talk me into coming out to the quarry tonight. I was going to get over this fear of jumping. Marc said if I finally jumped no one would pick on me anymore. He said that by coming to the quarry at night we could stay out as long as it took without me feeling pressured by anyone watching.

There's a reason he's my best friend.

We reached the quarry and threw our bikes down twenty yards from the edge. We stripped to our underwear.

Marc turned to me and smiled and then without one word he started running. He sailed off the ledge and seemed to hang in mid air with the moon behind him before he plummeted out of sight.

I heard a splash and then a whoop of delight.

"Are you ok?" I peeked nervously over the edge to see him climbing out onto the rocks below

"Come on, your turn. I know you can do it!"

I waited for him to climb back up, "I just don't think I'm ready for this, Marc."

"Listen, man, I know it's scary but you have to face your fear head on. You can't let fear control your life. I mean, it's ok to have a healthy fear of things that might hurt you but you've seen us all do it a hundred times. You have to choose to do it anyway. That's how brave men are born."

"Not you, you were brave from the minute you came into this world. You were born brave."

"That's not true. There's plenty that scares me."

"Oh yeah? Like what?"

"Like Mrs. Albertson!"

"Our science teacher?"

"Yeah, that mole on her schnoz is pretty scary but I still look her in the face every day, don't I?"

I laughed, "Hilarious, dumbass. That's not a real thing."

Marc stopped smiling and lowered his voice, "I'm scared of my dad."

I didn't know what to say. His voice sounded funny. I'd never heard Marc say he was scared of anything or anyone. I'd also never seen him cry. But now, even in the moonlight, it looked as if he had tears in his eyes.

"What? Why?"

"Look, you only know how dads are based on your own dad. Your dad is nice and play's ball with you and teaches you stuff. My dad isn't like your dad. He doesn't care if I exist or not."

"I'm sure your dad loves you in his own way."

"Maybe, I remind him of my mom or something. I don't know. But I don't think he loves me. Why do you think I'm at your house all the time? You don't even know how good you have it, do you?"

I didn't know what to say but I felt like I had to say something. "Why are you scared of him though? Has your dad ever hit you?"

"He doesn't beat me or anything but he isn't exactly the most loving parent either. I know how dads are supposed to be and he aint it. I guess he tries but he ends up yelling and then I yell back.

When he drinks it's like a switch gets flipped and all the anger he keeps inside boils out. I'm always worried it's going to boil out onto me. I have to walk on eggshells."

My dad had never raised his voice to me and hearing Marc talk about his dad this way made me nervous, "That does sound kinda scary."

Marc wiped his eyes with the back of his hand. "One of these days I wont be scared anymore and I'll stand up to him. Tell him how he makes me feel." Marc smiled and punched me in the shoulder. "Hell maybe I'll even do it tonight."

"Maybe my dad can talk to him? Help him see what a real dad is supposed to be like?"

Marc's face changed. "I'm not like you. I don't need someone to fight my battles for me."

I could see I had hurt his feelings but I wasn't sure what to do.

"I'm not a wimp. I can handle it just fine."

"I'm not saying you're a wimp. I just thought maybe your dad needs someone to talk to like another grown up or something."

"I only told you that stuff about my dad so you could see that everyone is scared of something but only wusses let it keep them from what they want. Stop being such a wuss and jump already! You let everyone make fun of you and then you think a grown up is going to fix it? Do you want to jump or do you want JT to keep smashing your face in?" Marc looked angry now. "Or maybe, you'd rather go home and tell your mommy you weren't really in a fight but that you were punched because you were too afraid to stand up for yourself?"

I stood up and clenched my fist. I had never felt like hitting anyone more in my life. Not even JT.

Marc looked down at my fist, "What are you doing, man I was just teasing. You want to punch ME now?"

"You never tease me, they tease me, you never do, that's why you're my best friend."

"Man, I'm sorry. I shouldn't have said that stuff."

My face burned with anger and I turned away from him.

"Hey man," he said, as he put his hand on my shoulder. I turned and shoved him so hard he fell on his ass. Marc looked up at me with regret and surprise. I didn't apologize. Instead, I straightened my back, turned towards the quarry and started running. When I reached the edge I just kept running, right out over the water.

My breath caught.

My stomach went into my throat.

I plummeted towards the water.

In that moment, I forgot everything Marc had told me about pointing my feet and holding my breath.

When I hit the water with a gigantic smack my mouth was open in a ginormous, soundless scream.

I went deep into the dark, cold, murky water. I opened my eyes but I couldn't tell which way was up. I resisted the urge to panic and let myself relax. I let my eyes focus on a dim light ahead of me and realized it was the big Montana moon getting closer as my body naturally rose to the surface. Once I broke the surface I gulped in the sweet night air and through the surging adrenaline roaring in my ears I could hear a voice in the distance, quickly getting louder. What the hell was that?

"Woo hoo!! You re a badass!! Geronimoooooooo."

All the way down Marc hollered culminating in a righteous

cannonball right next to me. When he came up he was laughing. He splashed me and I dunked his head under water.

"Man, I can't believe you did that!" Marc beamed.

"Well, you pissed me off!" I slapped the water towards his face in play anger.

"So, pissing you off is the only way to get you to say 'screw it'"?

I laughed, "I guess so."

"Right on!"

"Just don't do it anymore."

"I wont. I'm sorry. Forgive me?"

I reached over and dunked Marc again.

Chapter Three

Thirty minutes later, Marc and I stretched out on large towels and stared up at the starry sky.

"Tell me a story."

Marc was good at story telling. He loved to tell them and I loved to hear them.

"Once there was a boy from a small town."

"You always start off that way."

"Ssh. Once there was a boy from a small town, his name was Tony.

Tony wasn't particularly smart nor was he dumb. He might not have been book smart but he had an imagination and with imagination he knew could foresee all the things that could happen to him if he could just leave this small town. He liked the town he lived in just fine. He had friends there...." Marc stopped, looked over at me smiled. He looked back up at the sky and continued. "...but Tony knew there was much more out there. Other towns. Other friends. Tony knew he could travel to Egypt and make friends with a Sheik and become his personal bodyguard. He would tame tigers and eat grapes fed to him by harem girls."

I laughed at the image of Marc sitting in his tighty whitey's getting grapes dropped into his mouth by a bunch of girls.

Marc ignored me. "Tony also knew he could travel to the big city and become a broker on Wallstreet. He'd become so rich he would build a skyscraper just for himself. The building would be so high that it reached into the clouds. Airplanes would fly by and he would wave to the pilots from his window."

I gulped audibly and Marc laughed. My fear of heights, even though conquered momentarily, made me cringe at the thought of such a high building.

Marc continued, "Tony thought maybe he would travel to the jungles of the amazon and discover a tribe that would make them their ruler and they worship the ground he walked on.

One day, Tony got tired of dreaming and imagining and decided it was time to start doing. He packed his backpack with only the essentials, food and warm clothes and comic books."

"Comic books? Who takes comic books on an adventure?"

"Tony knew that traveling to distant lands took time so he needed something to read"

I laughed, "Fine, Tony took adventure ON his adventure."

"Do you want me to finish the story or not?"

I used my best British accent, "Please, continue your highness."

"Ok. With no money in his pocket Tony set off down the road. He tried to hitchhike but no one really wanted to pick up a kid in the middle of the night. He hid when he saw a cop car come by. He didn't want to get arrested and brought back home. Finally after walking all night and being so cold, a trucker stopped and asked him if he wanted a ride.

The trucker was a nice old codger with a red trucker hat that said 'Dreamscape'. Tony knew the hat was a sign so he got in. The trucker asked Tony where he was headed and Tony told him, 'I'm going as far as you are.'

'Well kid, I'm traveling all the way to the Indian ocean.'

'Sounds good to me,' Tony replied.

Soon the rumbling of the road caused Tony to fall asleep. It was so soothing and he was so tired.

Tony must have slept for hours because when he awoke he found himself on a ship!"

"How the heck did he get on a ship without even noticing? Did the old man carry him? Was he drugged?"

"Geez just chill. I'm getting there. Not everyone drugs you, you know."

"Whatever. All I'm saying is that there's no way I wouldn't notice being put on a ship…unless I was drugged."

Marc ignored me and continued, "So Tony found himself on the deck of a large ship. It looked like a pirate ship. Only not like pirates in the movies. These guys had guns and bandannas covering their faces. They put him to work swapping the poop deck."

We both laughed at the thought of this. I rolled around laughing and clutching my stomach. "Poop deck! There's no such thing."

"Shut up and let me finish my story," Marc laughed.

"So there I was, er there Tony was, swabbing the poop deck."

I squashed another wave of laughter.

"And suddenly the door to the belly of the ship opened with a bang. It was the captain. He had two real eyes, no eye patches and no parrot. But he did have a wooden leg. He grabbed Tony and yelled, 'A stowaway!' Tony was only a little scared but then the head pirate said, 'I need a right hand man. I just had to kill the other one. Are you up for the job?'

'I sure am,' said Tony. And so the pirate made Tony his best mate and they sailed on to Fiji to start plundering the islands for treasure."

I interrupted Marc, "Do you really want to stow away on a ship? You can't really want to be a pirate?"

"When I'm old enough I'm going to hop a train and ride the rails all the way to New York City!"

I had heard all of Marc's imaginings before but there was something magical about hearing him describe his wished for adventures. I knew I'd never go on any but it was fun to follow along in my head. It was like reading a book or having your best friend read a book to you out loud.

I started to have a sinking feeling in my stomach. One day Marc was going to leave and he would be leaving me here all by myself. I didn't like to think about that. I wasn't enjoying his story anymore. Now all I wanted to do was go home.

I stood up, "Come on its getting late."

Chapter Four

MARC AND I RODE HOME IN SILENCE AND WHEN WE REACHED MY driveway we hopped off our bikes. I dropped mine on the lawn where it had been before our escapade and started towards my moms daisies and my bedroom window.

"Hey man, wait."

I looked at Marc over my shoulder.

"Man, about what I said about my dad…"

"No worries. I won't say anything."

Marcs face lit up with relief, "Thanks bro."

I watched Marc ride off toward his house until he was out of sight. I climbed back into my room, and decided to leave the window opened for the first night in my life.

I climbed into bed and lay there staring at the ceiling. I couldn't stop smiling! I had done it! I had conquered my fear. I don't know what I would ever do without Marc if he ever decided to become Tony for real and leave this town. If Marc hadn't pushed me, I might never have gotten over my fear. And JT, that guy was never going to intimidate me again.

I turned on my side and within seconds I was asleep. I slept like

Tony; like someone drugged. When I woke up in the morning I wasn't on a ship but my world was definitely about to change.

Chapter Five

Roland, California
Present day

"FOUR-LINCOLN-SIX...", THE DISPATCHERS VOICE CUT THROUGH the silence in my patrol car. I picked up the mic to answer her, "4l6 go ahead."

"4l6 respond to a suspicious circumstance, audible alarm at 213 south 4th street. Glass breakage on the front window."

4L6, copy. En route. Code four." I'm not too far away from the address the dispatcher has given me and an alarm call at the local footlocker isn't exactly emergency business. This call is one I go to almost on a nightly basis.

I'm almost off duty and hopefully this will be the last uneventful call of an uneventful night shift. Being a cop is full of excitement but some nights are boring. Tonight, nothing exciting happened and with only an hour more to go I'm content to drag this call to OD time. I'm ready for the weekend.

Typically, a call of front window breakage just means some

homeless person ran into the door with their cart or some kids were walking through the storefronts trying doors. Easy peasy. I took my time getting there.

I pulled into the shopping center and killed my headlights. On the off chance someone had decided to break into the store I didn't want him or her to see me coming. I found a spot to park at the back of the store and got out of my car. I left the car running and the radio turned down so the would-be-burglar wouldn't hear it and get spooked. I tucked my baton in my keeper and donned my leather gloves. I grabbed my maglight from my sap pocket and held it in my off hand with the large beam pointed at the building.

I walked to the front of the store and examined the front door. The bottom half of the glass was shattered. Ok, so maybe someone WAS inside. "416 I've got an open door. Route me a cover unit and a k9 if ones available."

"Dispatch copies."

Dispatch assigned two more units and a k9 and I stand by waiting for my cover. I'm not rookie. Going in to check for burglars on my own isn't something I'm stupid enough to do.

I hear movement inside and key my mic again. I whisper into my mic, "I've got movement. Step up my cover." Not even 60 seconds later my two partners have pulled up out front and join me at the front door. I direct one officer to take the rear of the building and when the k9 shows up we let him take the lead.

The k9 gives the standard warning, yelling loud enough for any passerby's to hear that the k9 will be used to search the building and anyone inside better give up now. When we receive no response the handler goes in first and I'm right behind him. A third officer follows behind me and covers us both.

The store is your standard shoe store, small and u-shaped with the desk in the front. As we make our way behind the dog, my gun is out and at the ready. My adrenaline hasn't even jumped a tick. I'm used to this.

After ten years on the force, I've been on enough of these calls to be used to it but not complacent. I just know how to control it now. Breathe in and out. If you control the breath you can control the adrenaline. Focus on what's in front of you. Expect someone to jump out at any moment and know what you will do when it happens. By doing this over and over for years, it has become second nature and I'm not rattled in the slightest.

We clear the front of the store but find no one. I key my mic and let the officer out back know to keep an eye on the door as we are searching the stock room. That back door will be the only way out if someone tries to escape.

The back room is even smaller than the front of the store and it only takes us moments to search. The dog hasn't alerted yet but he keeps doing his job, ignoring all the yummy shoes to chew on. When the k9 handler gives the all clear I key my mic and let the rear cover officer know he can let it go. We are all good. No bad guys found.

I find the switch to the stores interior lights and flip them on. I tell my comrades I'm "code four" and they can go back to their own beats. I ask dispatch to call the storeowner and let them know I will be out front waiting for him to come secure his store.

I bring my patrol car to the front of the store and wait. Its only about fifteen minutes until the owner arrives and in that time I am able to knock out two reports I've been putting off writing.

The owner arrived and he and I do make a quick walk through of the store before he tells me it looked as if nothing had been stolen. He the storeowner tells me there is plywood, a hammer and nails in the back and I wait by the cash register while he goes to retrieve them.

I hear a crash from the back and this time my adrenaline hiccups.

I yell out, "Are you ok, sir?"

No response.

I keep calling out as I make my way to the rear of the store. Maybe he's fallen and knocked himself unconscious? I get to the stock room and walk into the office.

Holy shit!

Chapter Six

A MAN HOLDING A LEAD PIPE IS STANDING OVER THE BODY OF THE storeowner. My adrenaline is finally doing what it's supposed to and I forget to breath. I register the open roof hatch and the open safe. This asshole must've been hiding on the roof the whole time!

I draw my gun and order him to drop the pipe. He looks like a scared tweaker. He takes a step towards me and I keep yelling, "drop the pipe!" Pipe man pauses. Everything starts to happen in slow motion.

I key my mic and ask for my cover to return and make sure I add, "I've got one at gunpoint." Even from the storeroom I can hear the sirens starting up across the city, the sound bouncing off the fog. The adrenaline is rushing and my focus is on the man in front of me. I know my partners are coming but right now it's just him and me.

Pipe man drops the pipe.

"That's good. Now put your hands on your head and interlace your fingers."

Pipe man does as he's ordered.

"Drop to your knees."

Pipe man complies, slowly. I watch as pipe man reaches the floor but as he does he reaches one hand towards the contents of the open floor safe.

A gun.

"Don't do it!" I yell.

Slow motion. The pipe man's gun comes up and we fire at the same time. The gunfire rocks the small room and the ringing in my ears never seems to stop.

I've pulled the trigger three times in the course of my career and each time it's the same thing. Time stops. Every sound is muffled. My eyes see only what's in front of me.

I shake my head to gather my bearings. Tunnel vision will get you killed.

Pipe man doesn't move from his spot on the floor. A pool of bright red blood begins to outline his still frame.

I mentally assess my own health. I'm not hit but he is. He's gone down with three holes in his torso.

DAMMIT. Not again

Chapter Seven

"CAMDEN, WHY THE HELL DO YOU KEEP SHOOTING PEOPLE?"

"Captain, in my defense he was shooting at me first."

"Yeah, I get that but this is your third officer involved shooting in six months and now all eyes are on you. Do you know I have the press hounding me about you? I can see the headlines now: Renegade cop does it again!"

"Sorry Cap, I'll try to keep it in my pants next time someone tries to kill me."

"Oh you'll do more than that! You're gonna leave it on my desk!"

"What?"

"You're on administrative leave starting now, with pay so don't get your panties in a ruffle."

"For how long?"

"For as long as it takes for the DA to conclude its investigation."

I hear my voice take on a whiny tinge but I can't help myself, "You know how these investigations go, Captain. They could take months."

"They take as long as they take."

"But I didn't have to take time off the last couple times. Why this time?"

"Listen Jason, you need a time out. Get out of the public eye and scrutiny. Let things cool down. Let them do their investigation and prove this asshole did what you say he did. I know it's a clean shoot but kid, you need a break from us as much as the rest of us do from you."

I huffed like a twenty-eight year old toddler, "Those other two were clean shoots as well."

"I know they were. You were investigated and cleared but I think there's another issue at play here."

"What's that?"

"Your first shooting; I think you know what I mean."

"That's not fair."

"You're right. It's not fair. What happened was horrible but I think you're still trying to deal with it in your own way and that way isn't working."

"So you think that my first shooting is tainting the way I do my job? The shrink cleared me."

The captain didn't even blink. "Take a breath, son and listen to what I have to say. That first shooting was awful. It would be awful for any cop whether they had thirty years on or two. You had to take a man's life in order to save a kid. You did the right thing but you don't need me to tell you that.

What you need me to tell you is that in that situation it was traumatizing. You want to tell me you don't see that scene over and over in your mind when you go to sleep at night? You don't see that kids scared eyes looking at you in your dreams? You internalized it weather you realize it or not and there is something inside of you that is finding ways to get in that situation again."

"This city is dangerous. I am proactive isn't that what the job is about?"

The captain rolled sat back wearily in his chair, "Yes but I need you to cool it off for a bit. You need a break. You are chasing hot calls, running head first to everything you can and shit is finding you fast. I could move you to another beat but that's not going to change what's inside you."

I could see I wasn't getting anywhere but I couldn't seem to stop myself. "What the hell am I supposed to do away from this place? It's my life, Cap."

"That's part of the problem. You need a life outside of this place, Jason."

"Doing what? Getting married? Having kids? Drinking and going to bars? Spending money I don't have like everyone else? Become a gym rat? That's not me. I need to be out here doing my job! This is my calling. This is what I'm paid to do. Being a Roland P.D. cop gives my live meaning."

"This department can't be your 'everything.' What if something happened to you and you didn't have this job anymore? What would you do? What do you think would happen to the department?"

I laughed, "It would go to hell in a handbasket."

The captain clearly didn't find me amusing, "No, it wouldn't. This department would keep on functioning the same way it does now. You think this place gives two shits about you? They don't! Officer Jason Camden is just a cog in the machine and they will keep on functioning without you. You are not indispensible or irreplaceable."

"Cold."

Seeing the dejected and angry look on my face he tried to soften the blow, "Look kid. You are a great cop. I'd love to have ten more just like you but the truth is you cannot make this place your home. You need friends and family outside of this place. Go meet a girl or better yet, go home and see your family." The captains voice was softer now, "Go home, kid."

"I haven't been home in 10 years, Captain."

"I know. It's time. As your friend I'm asking you, go take care of business. See your folks. See your old friends. Milk a cow. Ride a horse. Rest, relax, drink beer and camp out."

"You think I'll be on leave long enough to do all that?"

Fed up with me, the captain slammed a drawer. "Dammit Jason. As your captain I am going to make damn sure you get at least a month off. You won't take that time under your own steam so I'm going to do it for you. Now get the hell out of my office before I make it two!"

I stormed out of the captains office and went to the locker room. I banged my locker door and punched it. That didn't curb my anger and frustration so I punched it again. Why the hell was I so angry? He was just trying to help and everything he had said, well, I knew it was truth.

I also knew why I didn't want to go home. Too many memories there. Too much had happened. I hadn't seen my folks in ages and I knew they missed me. I missed them too but when I thought about home memories of Marc enveloped all the others.

Fourteen years had gone by and I had never gotten over his disappearance.

The department had become my family and then I had made excuse after excuse not to go home. I worked holidays so my buddies with kids and wives could be home. I worked swingshift so I didn't have a schedule conducive to dating. I worked as many dangerous assignments as I could and chased as many drug dealers and badasses as possible.

The captain was right. I lived my life on the edge on purpose. But it had nothing to do with that first shooting. I'm not even sure how it happened but I knew there was an anger or need deep inside me that could only be assuaged by the adrenaline I got from this job.

Now what would I do without it? Not be a cop anymore? That thought scared the shit out of me.

I grabbed my gear and took a quick look around the locker room. I couldn't imagine a world without this job.

So, I did was I was told.

I was going home.

Chapter Eight

TWO DAYS AFTER THE CAPTAIN THREW ME OUT OF HIS OFFICE I WAS on an early morning flight to the middle of nowhere; a.k.a. Harmony, Montana.

The non-stop flight out of Sacramento was virtually empty. There weren't too many people going this way and I didn't blame them. I found my seat near the back of the plane and as I settled in for the four-hour trip, I thought about what I was leaving behind s well as what I was hurtling towards.

I had avoided coming home for ten years! So much had changed for me in that time. Once I graduated high school I couldn't wait to get out of Harmony. I told myself that nothing exciting ever happened there, and if I stayed I would end up stuck and miserable with a handful of kids and mortgage I had to bust my ass to afford. California, with its promise of eternal sunshine, ocean breezes and bustling city streets had lured me into packing my bags, buying a train ticket, renting a crappy one room apartment and joining the police academy in the space of one week.

In the first year of having made California my resident state, I had a job that made more money in a month than I knew I'd ever make in a year back home. I made interesting friends, surfed on the weekends and soaked up the multicultural atmosphere with every breath. The highs of my current life could never be duplicated back in Harmony and while I missed my folks, I would be glad when this trip came to an end and I could hurry back to the hustle and bustle.

When my flight safely landed at the Oak County Airstrip, I made my way to the car rental desk. My pops had tried insisting on picking me up but a guy needs a car to get around and I didn't want him to be put out if I had to leave suddenly. The captain had told me I would be off duty for at least a month but I knew differently. The department always needed warm bodies and boots on the pavement so I gave him a week before he would be calling to tell me I was needed back.

At the car rental desk I was given a choice of vehicles and maybe it was the fact that I was home or maybe it was just my country boy pride but I chose the largest truck they had. It was summer and the snow had long melted but a guy could always justify a four-wheel drive here. Besides, Montanan's are notoriously unaccepting of Californians and I wanted to fit in not stand out. I would leave the convertible and sports cars to my home turf and be who I was supposed to be here, a cowboy. Maybe I could get through this visit with as little visibility after all.

The drive from the airport to town should have taken about thirty minutes but I drove slowly and soaked up the scenery. The Rocky Mountains were just as high and majestic as they ever were and the heavy winter snowfall had left the countryside green and lush. There were a few snowdrifts left on the highest peaks and suddenly I was aching to take a drive up into the cold air and hike through the towering pine trees.

Montana was beautiful but I loved living near the bay. Ocean breezes did battle with traffic smog, the noise was a constant and there were so many people you could never be lonely. In contrast, my home state was quiet, clean and you drive for hours and not run into another person if you didn't want to. The sky was clear, the air was fresh and I rolled down my window to inhale deeply.

I reached Harmony city limits and smiled at the sign indicating six thousand residents. The population hadn't grown at all since I left. I drove down the tree lined main street and took it all in.

I arrived at the center of town and stopped at the one stoplight blinking red. I sat for a moment and looked around at the families walking dogs and kids riding bikes with towels over their shoulders. No doubt they were off to the quarry to swim.

On my left, stood the small town library. Next to the library was the town hall and police station. If I turned left and drove another two blocks I would hit the local hardware store. That would have to wait. Instead, I turned right on to Hazel Street.

I slowed at number 305 and saw the little white house was a little rundown but for the most part identical to my memories. This had been Marc's house.

My brain automatically skipped back to that last night with Marc at the quarry. The night I had learned not to be afraid. The night Marc had never made it home.

A thorough investigation had been conducted but after a month the authorities had given up the search for my missing best friend. Not a trace of him could be found, not even his bike. I had been devastated. Was he dead? Was he alive? I think the not knowing had been the hardest part.

I wondered what kind of family lived in this house now? Did they know what had happened all those years ago? Did they have a young boy of their own who moved into Marc's room and made it his own?

I wasn't certain what had become of Marc's dad but back then, in the years following Marc's disappearance, he had almost drunk himself to death on several occasions. He had eventually had Marc pronounced legally dead and a funeral had been held four years later. I didn't attend. I had already made my move to California and didn't bother to come home. I couldn't. I told myself everyone would understand my absence because I was in the police academy and busy but the truth was that I couldn't stand the thought of burying my best friend; especially without a best friend to bury.

For all anyone knew, Marc was still alive somewhere. Maybe he had just finally hopped that train like he always dreamed of and was climbing Mount Everest right now? I had never really accepted that he was gone. I couldn't fathom how Marc could have just vanished on the ride home from my house and no sign of him was found. Not unless he had wanted it that way.

That night had changed my life forever. I had gone to bed that night so excited and full of hope and awakened to a nightmare. My best friend was gone. To this day it remained a mystery.

A fluttering curtain in Marc's old window woke me from my thoughts. Imagining I saw someone peaking out, I sped up and headed to my folks place.

Chapter Nine

MY STREET LOOKED THE EXACT SAME AS IT HAD TEN YEARS AGO AND as the darkness I had felt in front of Marc's lifted, nostalgia for home took it's place in waves. The few phone calls home had been few and far between. I had missed my folks and I had missed this house. I didn't realize how much until I pulled up out front of child-hood home.

I loved that my parents still together after 40 years. That was hard to find in the city but not as uncommon here. Here families tended to stay together. I was an only child and I never wanted to have siblings. I didn't feel like I had missed out on anything. Most of my childhood friends had tons of brothers and sisters and they fought over everything or had to share. Not me. I had all Ma and Pa's attention to myself and it showed. I wasn't spoiled per se but I was their late baby so I garnered a lot of attention.

My dad was home every night and my mom was a stay at home until I got older. When I had entered high school Ma had taken a part time job at the library just to keep herself busy. Despite both my folks working I was never lonely. I had Marc and he was as close to a brother as I could have ever wanted.

I had been happy and content. And then Marc went missing

and something inside me shifted. I had to get out. Maybe I was just doing it because it's what Marc always wanted. Maybe in my own way I was living out the life he had always wanted because he couldn't. Maybe I was searching for him in all the dark places just hoping to find him and prove to myself he hadn't really died but that he was out living it up. That maybe I'd come across him and we'd be friends again like no time had passed. Maybe the captain was right, maybe I needed my head shrunk.

Is everything ok?

I pulled up to the front of my childhood home and Ma opened the door. She came out onto the wide front porch wiping her hands on her apron. She hadn't changed a bit. My heart swelled and I got out of my truck and almost ran to the front porch.

Ma wrapped me in a big hug, "Welcome home, son."

"Hi ma."

She patted my cheek and kissed it for good measure. I held her at arms length and took a good look at her. She looked a little weathered but still beautiful with golden hair laced with silver. Freckles still spattered the bridge of her nose and her eyes were still the color of corn blue flowers; bright as always.

"You look good mom. You haven't aged a day."

"Well thank you, dear, but you look like you've seen better days; tired and much too skinny."

I laughed, "Gee thanks! Don't hold back."

"Well it's true. I'm glad your home. Some rest from that fast paced California lifestyle, some good fattening up and you'll be right as rain."

"Yes ma'am," I said picking her up and swinging her around. Coming home had been a good idea. Mom was right. The captain was right. I needed a little bit of home and I didn't even realize how badly until this very moment.

"Where's dad?"

"Oh he's at the hardware store getting another tool to fix that garage door."

"I swear, he's ben working on that thing since I left!"

"You know how your dad likes to putter. I think he just likes going down to the hardware store. Even on his days off he can't stay outta that place. She always was his mistress."

"Oh mom, you know there will never be anyone as important to dad as you, not even his tools."

"Let's stop yakking out here in the porch. Grab your things and take them to your room. I've got food on the stove. I'm making all your favorites."

"Thanks ma. I'll take a cup of coffee if that's ok?"

"Ok? This is your home too baby and you are welcome to anything in it. And you know where the coffee pot is."

I laughed. She was all about babying me and then when I come to expect it she shoves me back out the nest.

Chapter Ten

I WENT TO THE KITCHEN AND MADE A CUP OF BLACK COFFEE. I carried it with my bags to my old room.

I switched on the light, and set my cup down on the dresser. Mom had cleaned it but the old smells still lingered. Ma had washed everything and kept it spic and span. I guess she had been hoping for this visit for a long time

From my room I could hear her happily singing and banging pots and pans around as she set to making dinner. Happy as a clam.

I set my suitcase on the foot of the bed and unpacked my few belongings. When I was done storing my belongings in the dresser and closet I poked through my old desk and stared at the pictures on the wall. I found a picture of Marc and I, with our bikes, out front of the house. I unpinned the picture and took it with me to my bed where I sat down.

It still hurt all these years later not knowing what had happened to the friend I had. I propped the photo up against the light on the night table and laid back on the bed and with my hands folded under my head

I stared up at the ceiling. It was so quiet hear. I was so used to noises of traffic rushing but here those sounds were replaced by the sounds of birds chirping and wind in the leaves of the trees. The tinkle of children's laughter replaced the sounds of horns honking and people shouting. The smells of moms cooking, fresh cut grass and cow manure replaced the smells of burning oil, smog and Mexican food trucks. It was a lovely replacement and it wasn't long before I drifted to sleep on a sea of relaxation.

Chapter Eleven

I WOKE TO A DARK ROOM AND AT FIRST I COULDN'T REMEMBER where I was. I hadn't dreamt and that was also a first in many years. Usually I dream heavily. My dreams always felt so real; shooting my gun, the bullet making its way to the end of the barrel and then plopping uselessly on the ground while an unidentifiable evil attacks. The events in my dream always happen in slow motion, like running through quicksand, and the only thing moving at normal speed is the danger that I face.

Sometimes I dream that the bad guy has shot everyone around me and he's coming after me at full speed but I cant pull the trigger no matter how hard I try. I squeeze and squeeze the trigger so hard and I know its all my fault that everyone else is dead. I couldn't save them.

Every cop has these nightmares, or so I've been told. It's normal. It still sucked.

I switched on the light and walked into the bathroom to wash my face. My coffee cup remained half full and untouched. The coffee was cold but I drank it down in one gulp and splashed cold water on my face.

I changed into a pair of running pants, my running shoes and a sweatshirt. I crept quietly to the kitchen, careful not to wake my folks.

The kitchen was dark save the light over the oven, which illuminated a note from mom.

Didn't want to wake you. There is a plate in the oven for you.

I peeked in the oven and smelled deliciousness. My mouth began to water but first, a run.

I stepped out onto the front porch and into the cool night air. I inhaled deeply, jogged to the sidewalk and turned left down the moonlit street.

I jogged slowly at first, working out the travel kinks in my leg and trying to get my bearings. I sped up a little as I reached the corner and felt my stride lengthen as the cool clean air filled my lungs. Nothing moved. It was after eleven p.m. and the town was tucked in for the night.

A few houses had little lights on in the windows but not one car passed me. I jogged three blocks before I hit the end of the lane and I stopped dead in my tracks. I stared off down the lane and breathed harder than my little jog warranted.

I stood still for a moment contemplating my next move and then with nervous resolution I headed towards the quarry.

Chapter Twelve

TWENTY MINUTES LATER I REACHED THE QUARRY AND I NERVOUSLY ventured towards the spot where I had learned to be brave. A chain link fence now surrounded the jump spot. I walked the length of the fence and found a spot where the local kids had cut a kid-sized hole. I bent my six-foot frame down and squeezed through the hole. I caught my running pants on a ragged piece of fence and tore a small hole.

Dammit.

I touched a drop of blood on my leg where the hole bared the skin of my right thigh. Great. Home twenty-four hours and I am already going to need a tetanus shot.

I walked through the clearing to the jumping ledge and peered down at the dark water below. The water seemed closer than I remembered it.

"What are you doing?" A voice startled me.

I spun around to a flashlight blinding my vision.

The voice continued, "You planning on jumping?"

"Could you get that out of my eyes?"

The flashlight lowered to my chest. "Sorry, Officer Johnson, Harmony P.D. This here is restricted area."

"Kirk? Is that you?"

"Depends on whose asking. Do I know you?"

"Its me, Jason Camden."

"Well holyyyyyyy shiiiiit!" The flashlight clicked off and now I was blind. I blinked trying to get my night vision to return.

Kirk reached out and pumped my hand furiously, "Man, what are you doing home?"

I retrieve my hand from Kirks, "Came in this morning. Just home for a little visit. When did you become a cop?"

"What? You think you have a monopoly on a law enforcement career?" Kirk punched me in the shoulder with a hearty laugh. "After you left I farted around a bit. Went to college for a few years but it wasn't for me. Came home and had to get serious. Kid on the way. I actually started off as a state trooper and then brought law and order home a few years back. Man, how many years has it been?"

"A few. I heard you married Bridget Holloway."

"Sure did. When got knocked up she told me I better get my shit together so I took the test and I've been running these red white and blues ever since."

"That's great man. Congrats."

"Thanks. So, what exactly are you doing out here?"

"Nothing really, I just went for a run and nostalgia got the best of me. I came in here to check out the old haunt. When did they put the fence up?"

"A few years back some kids were drinking and diving, like we all used to do, only this time a kid drowned. The kid's dad and mom got all uppity about it and now they have the fence so they cant jump no more."

"I'm surprised it hadn't happened before now."

"No shit. Remember all those times we used to come here and you were too scared to jump?"

"I sure do."

"And then what's his face tried to kick your ass over it and you never came back again."

"JT."

"Yes! I wonder whatever happened to that guy?"

"I didn't stop coming here because of JT."

"Was it because of Marc? You were the last one to see him right? You guys came out here that night?"

"Yeah but he and I rode home. That was the last time I saw him."

"That's a bummer man. I hate to cut our reminiscing short but I need to get back out on patrol." Kirk turned his flashlight back on, "Um, seriously, you can't be in here. Can I give you a lift?"

"Sure. Thanks."

As we drove the distance home, Kirk grilled me about my job in the "big city."

"What's it like there?"

"Hot."

"Ocean breezes though so who could hate that?"

"It's not like that. Gangs, run down neighborhoods, drugs everywhere. It gets pretty wild out there."

"I bet you see a lot of action, don't you?"

"More than I care to," I lied.

"So awesome, man. How long are you here for?"

"Probably just a few days but we will see. I'm going to spend some time catching up with my folks."

"Awesome." Kirk pulled the patrol car up to the curb in front of my home. "Stop by the precinct some time and we will catch up."

I got out of the car and then before shutting the door I asked, "Hey, were there ever any leads on Marc?"

"Not that I know of. I think we had some light duty officer who got bored and look at his old file as a cold case for like half a minute back in the 90's but there weren't any leads to follow up on. I can probably dig it up for you if you want to take a look at it?"

"Really?"

"Why not? A little professional courtesy wouldn't hurt."

"Thanks I think I just might take you up on that." I shut the car door and kirk slowly pulled off into the night with a little friendly twirl of his emergency lights.

Chapter Thirteen

I WENT UP THE STEPS AND TRIED TO BE AS QUIET AS I WHEN I HAD left. A dark shadow spoke from the recliner in the living room and made me jump.

"Hello son."

I flipped on the kitchen light and couldn't hold back the grim that lit up my face. "Hey pops."

Dad stood from his chair, crossed to the kitchen and hugged me hard. I hugged him back and he held me a little longer than I had expected. "It's good to have you home boy."

"Its good to be home dad."

"You want something to eat? You missed supper."

"Why didn't you wake me?"

"Mom was worried about you and wanted to let you sleep."

"Sure pop, I'd love something to eat."

I took a seat at the tiny kitchen table and watched as Pop heated the leftovers Mom had kept in the oven. It smelled so good. Fried chicken, mashed potato's and green beans straight from mom's garden. Heaven. My dad made himself a cup of warm milk and watched me as I ate.

"Did you go for a run?"

"Yes. I know it's a little late but I woke up and needed to work the kinks out."

"How was it?"

"Good. I almost forgot what fresh air smelled like. Town looks the same. Nothing seems to have changed."

"It has but not so as you'd notice much was. Was that Kirk Johnson dropping you off?"

"I ran into him down by the quarry. He gave me a ride back."

"What were you doing down there?"

"Remembering, I guess. There's a fence around it now. I guess he was patrolling the area when he found me. We got to talking. Kinda funny running into an old friend like that on my first night back."

"I don't remember you two being friends as kids."

"We weren't, really. He was a couple years older than me but I remember him."

"He married that Holloway girl and they have a daughter now."

"He told me." My fathers face had a disapproving look on it. "What's the matter Pop? You don't sound like you like him too much."

"He's a bully."

"How so?"

"He throws his weight around and rules with an iron fist."

I laughed out loud. "Now pops, cops are kinda just like that."

"Are you like that?"

"Sometimes. When I have to be."

"Harmony is a far cry from the city of Roland."

"True but cop work is cop work and sometimes you have to put your boots on and then down on someone's neck to get them to behave. You don't have any big problems here do you?"

"No."

"Well maybe some of the reason you don't is due to the fact that Kirk a little bit of a bully."

"Maybe. I still don't like him."

"It's ok, pop. You don't have to like everybody. Isn't that what you always told me?"

Pop sat there silently as I cleaned my plate. I poured myself a cup of cold coffee from the pot and warmed it up in the microwave.

"Won't that keep you up?"

"Not a bit. I'm used to it."

"Suit yourself. I'm going to bed. It's way past my bedtime. Would you like to go fishing with me tomorrow?"

"I'd love that! Can you take time away from the store?

"I'm the boss, aren't I? I'll be up early and off to the store so just sleep in and then head over to the store when you're ready. We can load up and head out from there. No rush."

"Ok, Pop." He kissed me on the top of my head before heading upstairs

Chapter Fourteen

I TOOK MY LUKEWARM CUP OF COFFEE AND WENT OUT ONTO THE front porch. I sat on the porch swing and stared into a sky full of stars. The crickets and coyotes seemed to be singing to each other. An then, amongst the noises of the nightlife, another sound. A twig snapped and immediately I was on high alert.

My hand instinctively went to my hip but my gun wasn't there. Shit. It was on my captain's desk. I hadn't traveled with my back up. My mind went to he gun rack in the living room. Dad had his hunting rifle there and a pistol. I tried to calm my overactive imagination. This wasn't the beat.

I took a shallow breath and listened. Nothing. I rose from my seat gently and walked to the porch edge. I peered into the dark straining to make sense of the night shadows. Was one of those shadows moving? Possibly but the shadow could be anything. I held my breath, willing myself to see clearly into the night. I jumped as a raccoon came lumbering out of the shadows and I laughed out loud. "Jerk."

I dumped the rest of my coffee over the rail into the yard and went inside. I locked the front door behind me and took one last peak out of the curtains. The raccoon had lumbered off into the neighborhood and there was still nothing to look at.

I took myself to my room. I wasn't sure id be able to sleep after my nap today but I was wrong. I conked out.

Chapter Fifteen

THE NEXT MORNING I WOKE AND FOUND POP HAD ALREADY LEFT FOR the hardware store. I enjoyed a leisurely breakfast with Mom. She seemed light and airy today and I think having me home has made her smile more. At least that's my story and I'm sticking to it.

After breakfast I took a light jog around the block breathing in the fresh pine smells and letting the warm Montana sun feed me the vitamin D I have been neglecting.

When I was back in my own yard I took a look around yard. In my head I knew that the raccoon had been the reason for my jangled nerves last night but my cop heart couldn't help itself. I went to the side of the house and poked around in Mom's flowerbeds. That's where I found it.

A footprint. A rather large foot print. It could have been an old one but the dirt was soft underneath. Maybe Dad had been out here this morning? I'd have to ask him when I got to the store. I tried to shake off that little unsettling feeling that was taking up residence in my stomach. I was sure I was over reacting.

I took one last glance around the yard and surrounding houses with curiosity. Nothing seemed out of place and the weird feeling of dread started to dissipate like one of my bad dreams. This was Harmony. I had nothing to fear.

I went inside and showered. I dug around in my closet and found my old fishing hat. It still had all the lures dad had stuck on it and faintly smelled of old lake water. I had worn this cap on every fishing trip dad and I had ever made. From the weeklong trips to catch the salmon as they spawned to the long lazy days down in the local creek; this hat and my dad had been the constants. This hat was a treasure.

I gathered dads and my fishing gear and packed it into the back-seat of my rental truck. I smiled like a teenager as the engine roared to life with a throaty roar. I missed having a truck. It didn't make senses to drive one in Cali where gas was five dollars a gallon but here I could get away with it and it was worth it.

I made my way downtown and stopped at the local diner to grab some sandwiches for the afternoon trip. Bojangles Cafe has been the local town hangout for over fifty years and I am certain the only thing that has changed is the ownership. It still had a sparkly red sign on the outside with a giant cowboy boot that rocked back and forth. Breakfast lunch and dinner were served at all hours of the day and the prices were the cheapest in America. Aside from the local church, Bojangles is the one place you went to know what was happening.

The cafe wasn't the only diner in town but by far the communi-ty's favorite. I think every kid who had ever lived in Harmony had slung at least a few shifts of burgers and fries here. From the small parking lot I could smell the delicious mix of frying potato's and fresh baked apple pie.

I entered through the old wooden front door and took a seat at the counter. The jukebox played a little Merle Haggard at an acceptable volume. In the evening they would turn the sound up but for now it made a nice backdrop to all the patrons gossiping.

A pretty blonde behind the counter had her back to me. She spoke over her shoulder, "Go ahead and take a seat anywhere. Ill be with you in a moment."

"A moments too long sweet thang," I twanged in my best hill-billy voice.

The blonde whirled on me but her angry face quickly turned to delight! "Oh my gosh! Jason Camden! Is that really you?"

She jumped over the counter right into my arms and I almost fell over. "Jeez Shelly, you always just go throwing yourself at men like that?"

Shelly Franklin, blonde bombshell extraordinaire, laughed as I set her on her feet, "Only when they are handsome as you. When did you get into town?"

"I flew in yesterday afternoon. I guess that small town gossip chain has lost its edge."

Shelly stuck out her bottom lip in a feigned pout, "and you didn't even call to say you were coming."

"Awe c'mon now Shelly. You know I'm no good at keeping in touch. Besides I didn't think you'd care if I was home or not seeing as how you married to that old, ugly bastard Ben."

"Who's calling me a bastard?" A voice boomed from the kitchen.

Shelly yelled back, "Just some young handsome thing trying to get me to leave you, honey."

Ben Franklin (oh the teasing he got as a kid) pushed through the swinging kitchen doors and laughed out loud. "Camden!" He came around the counter and wrapped me in a huge bear hug. He clapped me on the back, maybe a little too hard. "Man its good to see you! How long has it been?"

"Too long apparently." I patted his beer belly, "Looks like you've been drinking without me."

"It's all the good home cooking the little wifey has been doing."

Shelly rolled her eyes. "Please, I can barely boil water. But I can serve you a piece of pie like a rock star! Sit down and I'll cut you a slice."

"Just coffee for me, Shell. Dad and I are going fishing and I thought I'd pick up some sandwiches and stuff for lunch. You have anything already made?"

"Sandwiches? Psh. Ben's got some fresh made fried chicken, biscuits and coleslaw all cooked up. I'll pack you guys a nice lunch." Shelly retreated back behind the counter and Ben plopped down on a stool next to me. I punched Ben in the shoulder. "So what's the newest?"

"Not much, man. You know how this place is, not much changes around here."

"I see that Kirk Johnson is now a local cop?"

Ben laughed. "Yeah that guys a tool. Nice enough but he likes to boss people around. You know the saying 'you can't be a prophet in your own town?' Well not too many people take him seriously. Did you have a run in with him?"

"No, nothing like that. I just went for a run last night and ran into him out at the quarry."

Ben's face took on a sad look, "A little run down memory lane?"

"I suppose. It's hard not to think back to those times when I'm home."

"Marc was a good dude. He always stood up for everybody."

"True. Kirk says no one has made heads or tales of Marcs disappearance."

"Yeah it seems like after the initial fuss nothing happened and then Marc's dad had him declared dead. I think that made it feel kinda final in a way. You were questioned in that case weren't you?"

"I was supposedly the last person to see him. We went swimming that night and then he rode off for home."

"So sad." Ben hung his head.

I didn't know why I was talking about Marc but I couldn't seem to stop myself. "I went by the house on my way in. Is anyone living there?"

"Marc's dad still lives there. Never moved."

"Do you think his dad could have had anything to do with Marc going missing?"

"His pops? Old man was torn to hell when Marc went missing. I don't think anyone grieves like that if they had something to do with their own child's death."

"Who said Marc was dead?"

Ben looked at me warily, "Well shit, after all these years you think he isn't?"

"I suppose somewhere inside I've held out a little hope he was alive somewhere. Hitchhiking across America, seeing the sights. You know, living adventure after adventure."

"Maybe that's why his pop never left here. Still hoping his kid will come back."

"Maybe." I picked up my coffee cup and took a sip. "Kirk said I could come by and read the old file. I was thinking of maybe just taking a look. A fresh pair of cop eyeballs couldn't hurt, right?"

Ben shifted uncomfortably in his seat. "Sure. If you think its worth the heartache." Ben glanced around the café. "Look man, I know its gotta be a tough thing but that was so long ago what do you really think your going to be able to find out. Besides, how long are you going to be here anyway?"

"What does that have to do with anything?"

Ben pushed his stool back and stood up, "I'm just saying, you don't think it's a little cruel to just show up after so many years, stir up a hornets nest and then leave back to your big city? Do you miss the action that much that you have to bring it with you?"

I was stunned by Ben's reaction and I wasn't sure how to respond to him. "What's with all the hostility? I was just thinking out loud."

"No hostility, man. I'm just saying, some things are better just left in the past. If you're just here to visit, awesome. I want to see you and catch up but if you're here just to be super cop then don't bother wasting your time in here." Ben turned and started back to the kitchen.

I yelled after his retreating figure, "Ben! Ben, wait!"

Shelly came out the swinging door just as Ben pushed his way back through. She looked at me with a frown, "What was that all about?" She set a large picnic basket down on the counter with a thud.

"I have no idea. I was talking about Marc and he got upset and stormed off."

"Oh." Shelly looked down and sighed.

"What do you mean, 'oh?' You know what that was about?'"

"Jason, you have to understand. After you left and Kirk joined the force, Kirk reopened Marc's case. Kirk being Kirk, he brought Ben down and grilled him over the disappearance. It was based on nothing more than the fact that Marc and I had crushes on each other back then and now Ben and I were married. It was absolutely baseless. Kirk always had a thing for me and I think he was using it as an excuse to hassle Ben. Ben really took it personally. I mean, shit, we were fourteen for crying out loud."

"I'm sorry, Shell. I didn't mean to start any trouble."

Shelly kissed me on the cheek. "He will be fine. Give him about five minutes." Shelly smiled reassuringly and changed the subject. "You should come by tonight when your done fishing. That is if you don't have anything else going on?"

"Come by here?"

"Remember little bucktooth Jane Soren? Well she got her teeth fixed and now miss glamour puss is getting hitched. We are having a little party here. We are shutting the café down for the party and there will be a lot of friendly faces." Shelly did a little tap dance move and shoved her jazz hands in my face. "You could come get your shimmy, shimmy, shake on? Catch up with the old gang? Maybe meet a pretty little thing of your own?"

I laughed at her antics, "I'll think about it."

"You do that. I gotta get back to work. Kiss your pop for me. And if you boys catch anything, bring it by and we will put it on the menu."

I kissed Shelly on the cheek. "Thanks, Shell. Tell Ben I'm sorry, will you?"

"Don't think another thing about it."

I GRABBED the basket and headed out the door, letting the bells jingle softy as it closed behind me.

Chapter Sixteen

I FOUND A PARKING SPOT OUTSIDE CAMDEN HARDWARE STORE AND made my way inside. Dad had owned this store since he and Mom had married. Aside from his family, this store was his pride and joy. I practically grew up here. I spent all of my summers here. While everyone else was flipping burgers or smoking weed down at the drive-in I was helping my pop by stocking shelves and selling drill bits. Most kids would've complained but I loved every minute of it.

Pop was busy going over the differences of finishing nails and regular nails with a young mom with a baby on her hip so I made myself at home browsing paint swatches.

"Find one you like son?" Dad clapped a hand on my back.

"Hey, pop." I kissed him on the forehead. "You ready to catch some dinner?"

"Always. Let me grab my fishing stuff and make sure Shane is good to go. You know how these young kids are. He holds down the shop well enough but if I don't make sure all his questions are answered before I leave, he will be calling me non stop."

"Sure thing, Pop. I'll meet you out at the car."

I went outside and grabbed the broom leaning against the front wall. I started sweeping the sidewalk relishing the flood of summertime memories and old habits. While I swept up the dust, I hummed. I actually hummed while I worked! I don't remember the last time I hummed.

A loud commotion across the street caught my attention just as dad was stepping out to meet me.

"You little punk! Stop squirming." Kirk had some kid by the collar and was hauling him out of Mr. Gregson's drug store. The young boy of about twelve kicked him in the shin and Kirk howled but didn't let go of his little felon.

"Need some help there, Kirk?" I hollered across the street?

Kirk looked up and his scowl turned to a large grin. He waved with one hand while holding the squirming kid with the other. "Nope. I'm good! Little shoplifter here needs to be taught a lesson."

The boy squirmed, "Uncle Kirk, I said I was sorry!"

"You're lucky I don't whoop your ass right here in front of everyone!" Kirk opened the back door of his squad car and ushered the kid inside. "Your mom is gonna have your hide over this."

The boy began to cry as Kirk scolded him further. "You just sit here and think about what you've done and I swear if you open this door before I get back I'll put the handcuffs on you and take you straight to lockup. You here me?" Kirk slammed the door and after looking both ways he trotted across the street to shake hands with me and Pop.

Pop shook Kirks hand out of sheer politeness. "Looks like you have your hands full with that one, Kirk."

Kirk hitched up his uniform pants. "Just my nephew. He's been giving us a hard time lately and really acting out. Mr. Gregson caught him shoplifting so I came right over to make sure this is the last time."

Pop's face softened in sympathy for the boy. "Kids can be a handful at times. Maybe he is acting out for some reason?"

"I am sure you're right but a little discipline never hurt either."

Pop just couldn't help himself. "Sometimes too much discipline can do the opposite."

I looked at dad out of the corner of my eye. It wasn't like him to stick his nose in or his chin out but he had certainly decided today was the day.

Kirk seemed un-phased. "Yes, Sir." He turned to me. "Shelly told me she invited you to the party tonight. You coming?"

"I'll think about it."

Kirk took a quick glance at his nephew in the back of his patrol car. "Well good luck fishing and maybe I'll see you there."

Pop grunted as Kirk made his way back across the street. Turning on his overheads with a little dramatic flair Kirk drove away with his prisoner in tow.

Pop opened the passenger door of my truck and got in.

"You really don't seem to like him much, Pop. Did he give you a ticket or something?"

"I just think he's too big for his britches. Let's forget all about that guy and go do some fishing." He patted my arm. "I've been waiting for a gorgeous day like this all season. And now I get to spend it with you. Let's get cracking!"

I took the country road out of town and headed towards our favorite fishing hole.

Chapter Seventeen

DAD AND I FISHED FOR SEVERAL HOURS AND WHEN THE SUN GOT A little too warm, we stopped for lunch. As we were unpacking the picnic basket two men approached. Kirk was still in uniform but the police chief had on waders and was carrying a pole of his own.

My dad got up and shook hands with the police Chief. "Chief, afternoon!"

"Hi Bob. How is the fishing?"

"Not a nibble but the company is worth every minute." Pop motioned my way and I stood to shake the police chiefs hand. "Chief Jordan, you remember my son Jason?"

"I sure do!" He pumped my hand firmly. "I hear you went into the law enforcement business yourself, Jason."

"Sure did but I'm out in California these days."

"And, how's business out there?"

"Same as always; fast and furious."

The chief nodded in understanding, "Of that I have no doubt, son. If you ever think about leaving you just give me a holler."

Kirk frowned. "I didn't know we were hiring?"

The chief glanced at Kirk and then winked at me. "For you son I'd open another position."

I grinned in response. "Thanks Chief, I'll keep that in mind."

"Jason, I hope you will be staying for our annual Fourth of July carnival?"

"Not sure. I wasn't really planning on staying that long."

"It's only a week away. You came all this way to just turn and burn?"

I laughed. "Well, we will see. It's kind of open-ended trip but the department may need me back soon."

The chief studied me with interest. "Well, we hope you'll make it. There's a hell of a fireworks show planned and I hear your ma is going to be making her famous pies to sell. You don't want to miss those."

"No sir, I guess I don't. We'll see."

Kirk didn't smile at all. "The Fourth of July in Harmony is probably not nearly as exciting as the Fourth in the Bay Area, huh? You get a lot of calls and people shooting each other on the Fourth? Big money firework shows out on the bay? I can see how that would be hard to miss."

Maybe Pop was right. Kirk was a little obnoxious. "Well maybe a little home town celebration wouldn't hurt either, Kirk."

Chief Jordan seemed to sense this conversation was about to go sideways. He motioned to Kirk, "These fish aren't going to catch themselves." We all shook hands and I watched as both men walked down the shore. Well that was interesting.

Chapter Eighteen

POP AND I UNPACKED THE PICNIC BASKET THAT SHELLY HAD prepared and as we ate I thought about the footprint I had found. "Hey Pop, have you noticed anything strange around the house lately?"

Pop took a large bite of his fried chicken and sighed with delight. "Strange how?"

"I thought I heard a noise last night after you went to bed. I went out on the front porch but all I found was a fat raccoon. This morning I found a rather large boot print in the yard. Have there been any issues with transients lately? Anything suspicious?"

"Not that I'm aware of. The boot print could've belonged to anyone, son."

"I know but last night felt like someone was watching me. Someone other than a raccoon."

"Probably just those big city nerves getting the best of you. It was probably just a neighbor kid cutting through the yard on his way home."

Pop seemed unconcerned and I didn't want to start worrying him for no reason by pressing the issue. "You're probably right."

"Your to hyper vigilant, son. That city has probably got your nerves all jingle jangled. How's the job going anyway?"

"Jobs all good."

"Is that why you're here? Because it's all good?"

There had never been any sense in trying to hide things from my dad but I really didn't want to tell him all the dirty details of my latest invitation for time off. "Not exactly. I just had an incident and got some extra time off, that's all."

"Wanna tell me about it?"

I grabbed another piece of chicken from the basket. "Dad, you don't want to hear this stuff."

"Of course I do. I'm your dad I want to know what's happening with you."

"I got in a shooting." I snuck a peek at my old man out of the corner of my eye but he seemed relaxed.

"Were you hurt?"

"No, sir."

"Was the other person hurt?"

"He died."

"Did you have to shoot him in order to save yourself or someone else?"

"Yes."

"Then you did what you had to."

"I know, Pop. It's normal for officers involved in a shooting to be put on administrative leave during the ensuing investigation but my captain says I need a little more than time off. He thinks I'm struggling because of my first shooting."

Pop didn't say a word in response and I took it as my cue to continue. Pop was no shrink but maybe just talking it over with him would do something; break something free in me. "Pop, he was going to hurt a kid. I didn't have a choice." Surprisingly, my voice choked a little. Where had that come from?

"Tell me, son."

Dad was a man of few words but he was an excellent listener. I poked at my half-eaten fried chicken. "I went to domestic call. This lady was arguing with her husband and called for a civil standby. She wanted to leave him. He had been hurting her for years. She had finally gotten up the courage to go and she called for an officer to standby with her so she could get her stuff. I drew the call." I paused my story for a moment to collect my memories and form them into a palatable story my elderly father could stomach. "The husband showed up while I was there. I had my back turned for a split second and he grabbed one of the kids. A little girl. She was only six, Pop."

I glanced up at my fathers face but it betrayed nothing. I didn't really want to keep talking but the rest of the story came rushing out before I could stop myself. "He was holding her and had knife and the mom was screaming and back up was a ways away. I took the shot."

"Sounds to me like you saved that kids life, and probably her moms too."

I realized I was holding my breath and I exhaled slowly. "If I had been paying more attention, hadn't been so apathetic about him not being there, I would've seen him before he grabbed the kid. Then I wouldn't have had to kill anyone."

"Son, there's no reason to beat yourself up about what should've or could've been."

I threw my chicken down in defeat and wiped my hands on my jeans. There was no way I would be able to eat after this. My stomach churned at the memories. "Pop, I knew better. It was a rookie move."

"And you're telling me your captain believes that incident has tainted your most recent shooting?"

"Yes."

Pop put down his food and wiped his mouth carefully with his napkin. He took a deep breath and looked me in the eye. "Son, I can only imagine how hard it is to live with taking the life of another person. But you listen to me. What you are doing is important. You were sent there for a reason. That man holding that precious child hostage is the one who made the choice for you to kill him, not you. You had to react to the actions and choices he made and in turn you saved innocent people. "Yes, that little girl may be traumatized by the incident but that's not your fault. That's his fault, even if she never recognizes it. Even if your department or your city or your community doesn't recognize it, you did your job. What you did was heroic and you were brave to do it. It takes a lot of stones to do what you do.

I really had no idea how to respond to Pop's words of wisdom so I stayed silent.

"I always new you'd be a good leader."

I smiled. "You did? As a kid I was always afraid of everything! How could you know something like that?"

Pop touched my arm. "Not always you weren't. It took you awhile to find your inner strength but once you did, you used it. You followed your dream. You moved out of here and found a strong purpose."

"What if I was just running away?"

"So what if you were? It still takes strength to take a different path and not stay and wallow in what happened here."

Love for my Pop spread through my chest like wildfire. It didn't matter what I did, he would always be my biggest cheerleader. "Pop, I'm sorry I haven't come home more often."

"Don't you worry none about that. We miss you like crazy but I know you have a lot on your plate. And I also know that when your ready to come home, you will. Maybe this trip will help you realize that coming home will help. This is your soft place to land, son. This is where you come to heal from those things that you see every day. You just remember that."

"Have I told you how much I love you, Pop?"

"I know you do, son. I love you too. Now, we are just letting these fish get away with running amok. What do you say we catch a few and give your ma something to cook for dinner tonight?"

Chapter Nineteen

SEVERAL HOURS LATER, POP AND I PULLED INTO THE DRIVEWAY worn, sunburned and smelling like fish. We had finally put a dent into those fish "running amok" and we were both smiling from ear to ear.

We walked in the front door and mom yelled from the kitchen, "PEW! I can smell you both from here!"

Pop laughed. He reached for the fish I was carrying. "I'll take these in to your mom and you go clean up the tackle and put stuff away."

I went back out to the car, unpacked our fishing gear and stowed it in the garage. When I was done cleaning and stowing our gear, I took a look around the garage at all the stuff my ma had saved over the years. Neat and tidy but good gracious she didn't get rid of a thing, did she!

I moved a stack of boxes from the corner and found a treasure. My bike! Seriously? Still here after all these years? I sat on it and grimaced at the hardness of the seat. How had I ridden this thing summer after summer and not had callouses on my ass?

I pointed myself down the driveway and pedaled. They say you never forget how to ride a bike. While I hadn't forgotten how to ride, I had forgotten I was too big for this thing. Two pumps on the pedals and I lost control, crashing into the Camden family mailbox like a champ! Now I'm a twenty-eight year old, six-foot man with a skinned knee and bump on my head.

I looked up at the sound of tinkling laughter.

"Hey there Evel Knievel."

I got up and wiped my scraped up hands on my jeans. I stared at the vision before me. Maybe I'd hit my head harder than I thought.

"What were you doing, reliving your glory days?"

I stuttered like the fourteen year old who had owned that back. "Um, hi?" I was stunned. One of the most beautiful women I've ever seen stood before me in the warm afternoon sunlight. Red hair flying like a flag, brown skin with a smattering of freckles and wearing a white tank top under some baggy overalls. Yep, I'm pretty sure I have a concussion. She smelled like sunshine. I was speechless.

She put one hand on her hip and her green eyes twinkled with mischief. "Aren't you even going to give me a hug?

"Excuse me?"

The redhead smirked, "It's me, stupid. Sarahbeth Johnson."

"Little Sarahbeth? Kirk's sister? That's not possible. You're only six years old."

She sniffed a little in indignation. "I should think you would remember me for more than being Kirk's little sister."

"Sure I do," I say awkwardly. "I would hug you but I smell like fish guts."

Sarahbeth gestured towards the front of her overalls. "I don't mind, I'm full of paint anyway."

"Yes, you certainly are. What have you been doing, finger painting?"

"Cute. I'm painting a mural on the library wall and I was just finishing up for the day. I was on my way home when I saw you try to kill the mailbox."

I blushed. "You're an artist?"

"Something like that. I teach art at the high school. I also do art therapy with kids who suffer from trauma."

"That sounds very noble."

"It's worthwhile. I get to reach kids, help heal them with art. The act of creation is very therapeutic." Her eyes sparkled as she talked and I could tell she was passionate about her work. I wanted to know more but she changed the subject. "Are you coming to the party tonight?"

I looked back at the house. "I don't know. I'm only here for a bit and I've been fishing all day."

"You can take a shower and clean all that off you know?"

"Are you going to be there?"

"It's my party so I'd better be."

I felt my face betray my disappointment. "You're getting married?"

Sarahbeth smiled. "I'm putting it on. I'm the maid of honor."

Relief flooded through me and the red in my face started to dissipate.

Sarahbeth thread her arm through mine and let me up the driveway to the open garage door. "It'll be fun. Music, great food and good company. You really should consider it."

I was enamored with her freckles. They looked like a sky full of stars only more beautiful. I smiled back at her, "Well who could resist an invite like that?"

"Good. I'll see you at nine." With that, the redhead angel called Sarahbeth let go of my arm, kissed my cheek and then walked down the driveway and then down street.

I followed her scent to the sidewalk and picked up my old bike. Maybe this thing needed to go to Kirk's felon nephew.

I stowed my bike in the back of my truck and then went inside to shower and change. After a hot shower and I joined my folks a delicious dinner of fresh fish cooked to perfection. I couldn't believe how hungry I was even after the huge lunch Pop and I had shared.

Maybe confession was good for the soul. But so were redheads.

Chapter Twenty

After a dinner I checked my cell pone. I had been avoiding it since I arrived. This was the first time in ten years I had gone so long without my cell. I could see the message light blinking. What could it hurt?

Voicemails first.

There was a voicemail from Lizzie and hearing her voice made my heart ache for home. "Hey Jason. I was just calling to check on you. See how you were holding up. Don't worry about anything here, same old shit different day." Her voice paused momentarily. "Except for one thing. The DSVU sergeant came down and asked me if I wanted a detective spot! It all comes from this case I had the other night. Kidnapping, rape, car chase; I'll fill you in when you get back but I'm super pumped. When ARE you coming back? I miss you. Ok. Hope your resting and enjoying your time away. Don't call me back. Hide your cell and don't look at it until you are home."

I smiled. I missed her too. Lizzie and I had gotten to be really good friends after everything she had been through. She was a tough one. Pretty, heart of gold, sweet as could be and she had made her bones early on, the hard way. Not everyone at the department respected her for it. In fact several of them still talked shit about her and snubbed her.

I adored her. I had taken her under my wing early on and now she was definitely one of my best friends. I knew I could always count on her. She was my regular beat partner now that she was on her own but she had been off that night of my shooting. I was glad. She didn't need to see or be a part of that. She had a young kid. Sam. He was the awesomest. I know Lizzie is a cop doing the same job I am but I couldn't help it. Part of me wanted to protect her from the worst of it. She had been through enough.

The second voicemail was from the captain just filling me in on the investigation. Once I realized he wasn't telling me to come home, I didn't even finish listening to it. I just hit erase. I didn't need any of this work updates.

Several texts from my teammates and a few links to online articles about my shooting took up the rest of the messages but I could read them another time. I needed to get ready for this party. I could get depressed later.

I changed into some clean jeans, my old cowboy boots and a button up shirt. I grabbed my wallet and keys and left the phone. I grabbed my old cowboy hat on the way out and even spritzed on a little cologne. I felt silly but hey, redheads deserve someone who at least makes the effort. Besides, I wasn't entirely certain I had gotten rid of the fish smell.

I went into the living room, twirled like a moron and let my mother whistle at me. She kissed me goodnight and I told her and Pop not to wait up. I walked out to my truck with the sounds of Jeopardy floating through the open window and I felt happier than I had in a week.

Chapter Twenty-One

It was dusk when I arrived outside Bojangles Café. The outside lights were twinkling to the music rocking within. I had been forced to park a block away but the short walk in the fresh evening air was uplifting.

I entered the cafe and found the party was in full swing. I stood in the entryway for a minute and looked around at all the old familiar faces.

I felt a tug on my arm and found Sarahbeth standing close to me. She smelled like jasmine and she was wearing a little back dress to die for. I couldn't take my eyes off of her.

Sarahbeth ignored my ogling and pulled me towards the party-goers. "Come on, handsome, I want to show you off." She spent the next few minutes introducing me to those I didn't know and then when a slow song started up, she led me onto the dance floor. Sarahbeth unceremoniously threw her arms around my neck and danced a little too close. She was fun and sweet and the drinks were good and plentiful. I could feel a little buzz hitting and decided I didn't mind in the slightest.

The song ended and I led her off the dance floor to a nearby table where her friends made room for us. I let her sit and then asked, "Would you like a drink?"

Sarahbeth pointed her million-watt smile at me and I was mush. "Yes please."

I pushed my way to the makeshift bar and told Ben I needed two beers. Ben opened two bottles of cold beer and handed them to me. I tried to start up a conversation with my childhood friend. "Hey man, I'm sorry about this morning."

"Don't even sweat it, dude. I was having a rough morning, that's all." Ben handed me several cocktail napkins and I wiped the condensation from the bottles.

"Is there anything…" A drunken, angry voice interrupted me. "What the hell are you doing here?"

CRAP.

Chapter Twenty-Two

I SHOULD'VE KNOWN THIS NIGHT COULDN'T JUST BE PURE FUN AND relaxation. I turned around slowly. "Mr. Forrester. I'm home visiting. It's nice to see you." I stuck out my hand for Marc's dad to shake but he ignored it.

"Oh is it?"

He was going to make a scene. I tried to remain calm. The man was clearly still suffering after all these years and the smell of Jim Beam coming off him told me he had been drinking his feelings tonight. "Mr. Forrester you've been drinking. Let's go outside and talk."

"Well gee they ought to make you a detective, smarty pants. Anything you want to tell me, you tell me here in front of everyone." His voice had risen an octave and was getting louder by the syllable. "It's all your fault you lousy little shit."

Ben hopped the counter and quickly led Marc's dad towards the front door. Marc's dad was yelling now. "You were the last one to see him. What did you do to my boy? Where is my boy?"

Ben escorted Mr. Forrester through the door and out into the night. The music, dancing and party chatter continued as if nothing had happened but I could barely register it. After all these years Marc's dad still hadn't found closure. Could he really believe I had something to do with Marc's disappearance?

Sarahbeth made her way to my side. I think she could see I was slightly shaken. "Come on. Let's blow the dust of this place, handsome."

"But you're the maid of honor. Won't you be missed?"

"Everyone's so drunk they won't even notice I'm gone. Besides, you look like you could use some air."

"Lead the way."

I followed Sarahbeth outside and took a cautious look around. Sarahbeth nudged me with her shoulder. "He's gone. If I know Ben, he's driven Mr. Forrester home." Sarahbeth started walking down the block and I followed.

Sarahbeth took my hand. "Are you ok?"

"Yep. I'm used to getting yelled at back home. On the job I get yelled at several times a shift. In FACT, if I am NOT getting yelled at, I know something is wrong." I have a knack for glossing over uncomfortable feelings with sarcasm.

"But this isn't home and you're not working." Sarahbeth squeezed my hand tighter. "He doesn't really think that you had anything to do with Marc's disappearance, you know."

"No? Could've fooled me. It's been how many years and he still hates me? I guess he has to have someone to blame."

"Well did you?"

I stopped in my tracks and retrieved my hand from hers. "Sarahbeth, I had nothing to do with Marc disappearing."

Sarahbeth grabbed my hand back. "I know you didn't. You couldn't have."

We began to walk again and the silence between us was easy and somehow needed. We had managed to walk almost all the way around the block when she stopped me. "Maybe you could use a little art therapy?"

I smiled down at her innocent face. "You think so?" She put her arms around my neck and kissed me softly. "I could help you with that."

I swept a mop of red hair from Sarahbeth's face and kissed her back. "Oh young lady I am certain you could. But for now, lets head back to your party. I've had enough fresh air."

Sarahbeth and I continued to walk in silence, hand in hand until we reached the location of my truck. I stopped dead in my tracks.

Chapter Twenty-Three

"DAMN IT!!"

"Umm, tell me that's not your truck?"

I walked over to my ride and examined the shattered windshield. "Technically it's not mine. It's a rental."

Sarahbeth picked up a piece of glass from the sidewalk. "I hope you got insurance."

I rolled my eyes at her.

"Who do you think did this? Do you think it was Marc's dad?"

"I really have no idea.

Sarahbeth took out her cell and began dialing.

"Who are you calling?"

"Kirk. He can at least take a report so you can give the information to the insurance company. If you're lucky they wont hold it against you."

Kirk arrived within minutes and I may have been wrong but it looked as if he was pleased I had suffered a little vandalism. "Well what happened here?" Kirk walked around the rental truck examining it. He came back to our spot on the sidewalk and looked at Sarahbeth, "What are you doing out here?"

"Don't worry about what I'm doing out here. Just take the man's report, Kirk."

I kicked some loose glass on the sidewalk. "I came to the party. Was there for maybe an hour. I came out and the windshield was busted."

"You see anyone suspicious?"

"Nope."

"Anyone you can think of who might want to do this? Any enemies?"

"No."

Sarahbeth interrupted. "Yes! John Forrester showed up to the party and he was pretty drunk. He laid into Jason a little."

Kirk didn't even try to hide his smile this time. "Ok. Let me take down all your info." I answered all of the necessary questions and a few I was pretty certain were just for Kirk's amusement. Is this how all victim's feel at the other end of my own preliminary investigation?

When Kirk was done farting around he handed me a slip of paper with the report number written on it. "Stop by the station tomorrow or the next day and I'll give you a copy of the report you can take to the rental car company."

"Thanks I appreciate it."

Kirk just stood there with his hand on his gun smiling that dumb smile. I looked at Sarahbeth who was busy watching Kirk with an irritated eye.

I touched Sarahbeth's shoulder. "I'm going to head home."

"No! Come back to the party with me." Sarahbeth grabbed my hand but the look in Kirk's eyes told me it was definitely time to go home. It also didn't appear He was planning on leaving his little sister alone with me so a kiss goodnight was for certain out of the question. I took my hand back from Sarahbeth and began backing towards my truck. "I should go. It's been a long day."

"When will I see you again?"

Kirk took Sarahbeth by the elbow. "Jeez girl, leave the man alone. He's here to visit and relax not get mauled by you."

"Shut up, Kirk."

I wasn't entirely sure how to respond to Sarahbeth so I did the next best thing; I waffled. "I'm going to be pretty busy with my folks and I might even be heading home in the next few days. I'm not sure I will have a lot of time for hanging out."

"I see. Doesn't your mom work at the library?"

"As a matter of fact she does."

"Then that settles it. You come visit her at work tomorrow and while you are there you can take a look at the mural I'll be working on."

"Tomorrow is Sunday. Library will be closed."

Sarahbeth winked at me. "I'll be there painting anyway. West side of the building. Big pictures of books. Smells like turpentine. Cant miss me."

I smiled at her tenacity and she reached up and pecked me on the cheek. Sarahbeth turned and gave her brother a snotty look.

Kirk rolled his eyes again, "C'mon, little sister, I'll give you a ride back."

I watched as brother and sister drove away in Kirk's patrol car. What the hell was I doing?

Chapter Twenty-Four

I watched Kirk's car disappear around the corner. I swept the broken glass from the driver seat of my pickup and climbed in. It was going to be almost impossible to see through the windshield but maybe if I drove slowly enough I could get home in one piece.

Whoever had broken my windshield had done a great job. The rental company wasn't going to be happy about this. As I drove, I kept a careful watch in my rear view mirror. I had a feeling Kirk would use any opportunity he could to hassle.

Several times I thought I saw his patrol car in the distance but at this time of night, car lights could have belonged to anyone. Just as I had convinced myself I would make it home with no issues, a patrol car pulled onto the road behind me. I kept waiting for Kirk to pull me over but he continued to stay two car lengths behind me. Maybe he was just making sure I made it home safely instead of heading back to the party to snuggle with his little sister? I was a block from home when the patrol car turned off and drove off into town.

What a weirdo.

Chapter Twenty-Five

I parked the truck at the curb and didn't even bother to lock it. Hell, if someone wanted to steal it, I'd rather they didn't break another window to do so.

I stood on the front porch listening to the night sounds for a few minutes. I had no feelings of being watched like I had the night before and suddenly felt a little silly that I had even worried. Dad was right. I was hyper vigilant and needed to tone it down.

I opened and shut the front door as softly as I could. Mom and Pop were sleeping and I smiled at the sound of my dad's snoring gently making it down the hallway. Some things never changed.

I went to my room and after brushing my teeth and putting on my sweats I briefly considered going for a run. I usually went for a run before bed because it helped me sleep better but tonight, I was just too tired. Five minutes later I was tucked in under my fourteen-year-old Spiderman comforter. I lay on my side and looked out the window. The moon was nowhere to be found tonight but the sky was lit with a million stars. It was soothing. I was asleep in seconds.

Chapter Twenty-Six

I DREAMED. THIS ONE WAS A NEW VERSION OF AN OLD NIGHTMARE. The man came out of nowhere. He was dressed as a cop but in my mind, in my dream mind, I knew he was the bad guy. He grabbed the little girl and held the knife close to her throat. His face was expressionless but his eyes found mind and I stared into two black pools.

The bad guy looked familiar but in my dream state I couldn't name him. The man was silent but the little girl screamed and screamed. She had red hair and bright blue eyes full of terror. She was begging me to save her.

I pulled my gun. I pulled the trigger with all my might and nothing happened. I pulled again but it didn't budge. Not even a millimeter. The man began to laugh. His laughter mixed with the little girls cries for help and I could feel myself start to panic. I gripped the gun with both hands. I put two fingers on the trigger and squeezed with all my might.

BANG!

. . .

I AWOKE WITH A START, panting, covered in sweat and both my hands cramping. I kicked off the sheets, got up and flung open my bedroom window. I held my face to the screen and let the cook night air wash away the cobwebs of the dream.

An owl hooted and I jumped. Shit.

Once the sweat had dried and my heart stopped racing I climbed back into bed. I would not be sleeping any more tonight. I should've gone for that run.

I reached for my cell phone. Now was as good a time as any to check my messages and read the articles my co-workers had sent me. I turned the phone on and found a text from Lizzie.

Don't read your messages!!!

Relax!

I smiled in my darkened room. She knew me too well.

I changed my mind. Instead of scrolling through the rest of my messages I clicked off the phone and lay there controlling my breathing. I had learned some breathing techniques so I practiced them now. Some woo woo guy had come to the department during Advanced Officer Training and tried to teach us something called mindfulness.

For the most part it was crap but I had used the breathing techniques he had taught us. I found they were helpful during my shift when shit was hitting the fan, or when I woke p form a nightmare and needed to bring my heart rate out of the danger zone.

I lay my hand on my chest and breathed in slowly and deeply counting to ten. I exhaled slowly counting to fifteen. I did until I no longer saw monsters in the shadows and drifted slowly towards a peaceful oblivion.

Chapter Twenty-Seven

I WOKE UP LATER THAN USUAL BUT AFTER A RESTLESS NIGHT I WASN'T surprised. It was Sunday and my folks had already left for church. I was surprised Mom hadn't come in and shaken me, demanding I put on my best and join her in the family pew. I was grateful she let me sleep.

I got up and went to the bedroom window. For a moment I could picture that last night with Marc as if it was last night. I looked out the window and down at mom's flower beds. I imagined I could still see the impression I'd made with my clumsy fall into her daisies.

Lost in reverie it took me a moment to realize there were actual footprints in the daisies! I grabbed a shirt and went outside and looked more closely at the ground. Sure enough, in the damp earth were actual footprints, adult footprints. Just like the one I had found in the yard the other morning. My head was suddenly on swivel. I looked up and down the street, searching for someone who I was certain had been long gone.

Someone had been in the yard and this time it looked as if they had been looking in the bedroom window. The street seemed just as quiet and beautiful as always. Peaceful. Not one sign of anything dangerous but my cop senses were tingling. Something wasn't right.

Who was poking around here? I wondered if this was happening before I came home or if this was just for my benefit. I had to go to the police station this morning anyway to get my report for the insurance company so I'd make sure and ask about any prowlers. Dad had said it was no big deal but this made me nervous.

I went back inside the house, locking the door behind me

After a quick shower I headed towards the Bojangles in my miserable truck. I needed coffee and I needed answers. Nowhere better to find both.

Chapter Twenty-Eight

WHEN I ENTERED THE CAFÉ BEN WAS BEHIND THE STOVE AND Shelly was flirting her way among tables scattered with customers. Church was still in session and the café was only a quarter filled. I had my pick of places to sit. That's one thing about a small town; pretty much everyone was at church on a Sunday morning.

The smell of fresh cinnamon rolls and dark roast coffee made my stomach grumble and I was glad I had come in.

Shelly came to my table and set a large platter in front of me. It was piled high with eggs, toast, bacon, hash browns and grits with melted butter.

"Woman, do I look like I need fattening up? I didn't even order and you seem to know exactly what I would want, even if it is a little much."

Shelly sat down across from me. "Shut up and eat, Jason."

"Well good morning to you too sunshine."

"I have a few minutes in between customers. I heard about what happened last night."

I thought about Sarahbeth's warm hand in mine, and her soft lips kissing me in the starlight. My face blushed before I could stop it.

"Your windshield got smashed in?"

I almost choked on my eggs. "Yeah it was a mess."

"Do you think it was Marc's dad?"

"I have no idea. It could've been anyone really."

"What did the police say?"

"You mean Kirk? He said it was probably kids."

Shelly looked at me skeptically. "Really? Kids?"

"Yeah. Why? Does that seem impossible?"

"It just seems like a weird thing for kids to do. Kids don't usually go around breaking car windshields for no reason. At least not in Harmony."

"What are you saying? You think it was a personal attack on me?"

"Maybe."

"But why? I haven't been home in years. Who could possibly want to do something like that to me?"

"Have you been making anyone angry since you've been home? Who knows, maybe someone is jealous of your big city success?"

I laughed. "That's silly, Shell."

Shelly waggled her eyes at me, reached over to my plate and picked at my bacon. "Maybe someone saw you dancing with a certain redhead?"

I ignored Shelly's attempt to pry and I slapped her hand away playfully. "Hey I'm a growing boy. I need all the protein I can get."

The cafe door jangled open and a young couple walked in. Shelly got up with a sigh. "Fine. Don't tell me all the dirty details. I gotta get back to work anyway. But Jason, please be careful. Something doesn't feel right and I don't want anything to happen to you." Shelly patted my shoulder as she went off to greet her newest patrons.

As I ate my monster breakfast, I considered what Shelly had said. Could someone be targeting me? Why? Someone was definitely prowling around the house. Then there was the windshield. Marc's dad may have been responsible but it seemed he hadn't even known I was in town until last night.

My only option was to run things by Kirk and see if anything weird had been going on before I got to town. I finished my breakfast...yes, the whole thing....and after leaving Shelly a hefty tip I waddled off to the police department.

Chapter Twenty-Nine

IN AN EFFORT TO SPEED UP DIGESTION AND COMBAT GUILTY thoughts of what a glutton I had been, I walked the several blocks to the Harmony Police Department.

I took my time and enjoyed the tree-lined street. I glanced in the windows of the barbershop, its neighboring nail salon and window shopped at the old bookshop. I continued on past the park where kids were screaming and laughing while their parents watched from perches on benches or blankets laid out on the grass. Geese wandered everywhere and the man-made lake in the middle of the park was full of ducks showering in the fountain.

Lizzie and Sam would love it here. I wasn't really sure what made me think of them but this whole small town atmosphere seemed like it would fit Lizzie well. I missed her. A pang of…something…hit me and I stopped and sat on a bench. I couldn't identify what I was feeling but I knew if I called Lizzie I would be able to figure it out

The phone rang twice and then, "Hi!" Lizzie's sunshiny voice lit a smile on my face.

"Hey girl. You surviving without me?"

"Not even a little bit. Kronig has been working your beat and he's horrid! Every time there's a call he doesn't want to go to he pre-empts himself and makes a car stop! I end up having to take it. I swear, I've written more paper outside my beat since you've been gone than during my entire training!"

I laughed. "Tell me your big news. Your message had my interest piqued."

"Oh my gosh it was crazy! I will give you the long story short. You shouldn't be thinking about work AT ALL. But since you insist-ed." Lizzie giggled a little and it made me feel at home. "I on-viewed a kidnapping slash sexual assault and the guy got away. BUT, I got the car info and the detectives came out. They ended up catching the guy and then Sergeant O'Connell asked me if I wanted to be a detective when the spot opens up at the beginning of the year. But like I said, I'll tell you all about it when you get home."

Lizzie paused for a breath. "How's Montana?"

"First of all, good job! I can't wait to here all about your big case! Secondly, it's beautiful here. The scenery never gets old. I went fishing with my dad and we had a great time. You would love it here. Sam would be in kid heaven."

"Have you had a chance to catch up with any old friends?"

I thought about Sarahbeth and felt my face flush. Lizzie wouldn't care but I felt a little weird telling her about my one date. "A few. Mostly I'm just hanging out with Mom and Dad and enjoying the peace. If you can believe it, you're the only person I've talked to back home. It feels good to unplug."

"That's great! I'm glad you're getting a little away time."

I finally asked Lizzie what I really wanted to know. "How are things going back there? What's everyone saying about the inves-tigation?"

Lizzie didn't answer for a full two seconds. Two. Very. Long. Seconds. "Don't Jason. Don't do this. You went to Montana to get away from this. It doesn't matter what's going on here."

"Lizzie. I guess I'm just a little concerned about my job. You can understand that."

"Yes, I suppose I can. You know how things are going here. You've been through it before. Everything gets scrutinized, pushed out of proportion and then eventually it all falls into place. Please don't think about it."

"Part of me doesn't want to come back."

"I don't blame you but you better come home eventually. If you leave me stuck with this jerk of a beat partner I'll fly up there and bring you home myself!"

I laughed. "I miss you too, kid."

Lizzie laughed too. "I hate to cut you short but I have to go pick up Sam. I'm glad you called. You really are ok right?

I thought about telling Lizzie about the car and the footprints but stopped myself. Three tiny little incidents that were probably nothing do not make a case worth discussing with your partner who was 3000 miles away. "Yes, I'm better than ok. I'm great. Give Sam a fist pound for me will ya?"

"I will! See you when you get back."

I disconnected and tried to shake off the feeling in the pit of my stomach. I shouldn't have called. It just brought to forefront the shooting and the investigation and why I was here in the first place. I needed a distraction; some way to spend all this pent up anxiety. I got up and continued towards the police department. I knew just what to do.

Chapter Thirty

Minutes later, I entered the City of Harmony Police Department. The lobby was about one hundred square feet and sported one bay window with no safety glass. Pictures of every Harmony Chief of Police, since its inception, lined the dark wood paneling.

In true Montana fashion, a stuffed and mounted deer head hung on the wall. The buck looked as if it had also been there since the department's inception.

I went to the reception window and dinged the bell for assistance as the sign instructed. No one came. It was Sunday so I suppose I shouldn't have expected much. I called out, "Hello? Is anyone there?"

From the back I heard a male voice. "I'll be right with you."

Kirk came around the corner and smiled. "Well hey partner! Sorry to keep you waiting. Here, I'll buzz you back."

I heard a buzzer sound and the door next to me unlocked. I went in and Kirk motioned for me to follow him. I followed Kirk to what appeared to be a break room. A water cooler, a round table with a box of donuts, a coffee pot that smelled like it was burning and a TV turned to a rerun of Bonanza. Maybe this was Kirk's office?

Kirk grabbed a chocolate donut and took a bite. Around the mouthful of dough he asked, "What brings you by?"

"I wanted to get a copy of the report from last night?"

"Oh that's right, your car. I haven't finished it yet." Kirk ate another large bite of donut, crumbs falling on his chest and dirtying his uniform.

"How long will that take? I can come back tomorrow."

"No, no. Sit. I can write it up now. Won't take me more than a minute."

"I was wondering, could I look at that file while you write that report?"

"What file would that be?"

"Marc's missing person file. You said I could take a look at it?"

Kirk stood there munching his donut and staring at me. He licked his fingers and finally said, "Oh sure. I'll grab it for you." He really was a strange sort.

Once Kirk left the room I took the opportunity to look around a little more. Being nosy is in every cop's nature. I looked at the wanted bulletins on the board above the coffee pot. Amongst the missing cats and dogs was a flyer identifying the FBI's ten most wanted. I lifted the flyers listing wants and warrants from surrounding cities and read the wires concerning missing kids throughout the nation. I thumbed through the stack that seemed to go back years. I didn't find Marc's. I don't know why I thought it might even be there.

Kirk returned a few minutes later with a manila folder. "Sorry, we are a little short handed. Nothing really goes on here on Sunday anyway."

Kirk started thumbing through the file. "Not much here. Didn't look like we had too many leads. You sure you want to waste your time?"

I held out my hand for the file. "That's ok. I'm just curious. I'm not trying to solve anything."

Kirk looked at me for a long minute before slowly handing me the file. "Ok partner. Just promise me one thing; if you think you find something you check with me first. I don't want you going off half-cocked." Kirk walked toward the door but turned back at the last minute He pointed a chocolate covered finger at me. "That file doesn't leave this room. You got that?"

Kirk was stern, suspicious even. Not like the goofy Kirk I knew. His face suddenly broke into his signature grin and he slapped the doorframe. "Look at the two of us. Who would've thought it, huh? I'll make a fresh pot of coffee and then we can get to work, partner."

This guy might have a screw loose. I couldn't quite get a handle on his personality or multitude thereof.

I watched him make the coffee as I took a seat at the round table. After the coffee had started brewing, Kirk went into the next room. I waited until I could hear the clack of typewriter keys indicating Kirk was busy working on my report.

I found the TV remote and pressed the sticky keys until the sound on Bonanza was muted. I stared down at the file folder on the table in front of me. Was I really sure I wanted to open this? Why was I even here? This seemed so silly after all these years. The police had done an investigation and found nothing; no body, no clues.

What did I think I was going to find?

Chapter Thirty-One

I OPENED THE FILE AND THUMBED THROUGH THE STACK OF PAPERS that equaled a "thorough investigation." I cringed. It seemed pretty skimpy even for this small police department.

I found a copy of the original missing child poster that had been dispatched to police department's countrywide. My throat caught. Marc was only fourteen and he looked every bit as young and innocent as decade he went missing in.

I lay the photos aside and continued to read through the preliminary report. The initial statement given by Marc's dad had been made at 1000 hours on the morning after we had gone swimming.

On the morning in question, Marc's dad had gone to wake him to get chores done and found that Marc wasn't there. His bed hadn't even been slept in. His dad had been so angry that he had gone around to Marc's friend's houses looking for him.

I remembered waking up that morning to pounding on our front door and then Mom coming to tell me that Marc was missing. When I told Marc's dad that I didn't know where Marc was, he had called me a liar. My mom had tried to calm him but he had been so loud and rude that my dad, bigger and stronger back then, had ushered him out to the front porch.

I had snuck to the window and listened to muffled voices as they talked and Marc's dad had stalked off angrily. I had been too scared to tell to Marc's dad about our night swim I had waited until he left. Mom had understood and instead of calling Marc's dad she had called the police.

My trip down memory lane was brought to an end as the clack of the keys in the next room stopped. Kirk came in. "Hey, one question, do you have the paperwork for the rental car on you? I need to make a copy of it for the file."

I fished the papers out of my wallet and handed them to him. He left and I heard the whir of the copy machine warming up and then beeping as it duplicated my receipts.

I turned my attention back to the reading matter at hand. I read Marc's dad's statement, my one statement and the statements from the neighbor's.

Marc's neighbor, Marge Hollenbeck, had been interviewed. Marge had reported hearing voices arguing on the night of Marc's disappearance. According to the statement, Marge was certain the arguing came from Marc's front porch at approximately eleven p.m.

I rubbed my temples. Marge said that she heard Marc and his dad but I knew that at eleven p.m. Marc had just left my house. There was no way he could have been home by then. Marge must've been wrong. She had been ancient even back then.

When questioned about the argument, Marc's dad had said Marge was imagining thing's. Mr. Forrester said he had been in bed asleep by eight and hadn't woken until morning. The responding officer had reported a plethora of beer cans on the living room table and believed that Marc's dad had drunk himself into a deep slumber.

Marc's dad had admitted to having "a few."

I wondered who Marge might've heard? I wondered if she was even still alive? It wouldn't hurt to talk to her. If I could find her, that was. No other neighbors had reported anything. That seemed weird.

According to the reports in this file, Marc had disappeared without a trace. The police had searched his room and found all his belongings still there. They said the likelihood that Marc had run away without taking any of his stuff with him, was slim. His bike was never located.

The police had scoured the house and Marc's dad's car. They had gone door-to-door and house-to-house but nothing clues had been discovered. Police questioned all the kids we hung around with that summer. Because of the fistfight, JT got special attention.

Information spread around town that I had been the last one to see Marc and a few of the mean kids had even started rumors that I had something to do with his disappearance. It had hurt me deeply.

Marc's picture had been shown all over the news for weeks but then, as typically happens in small towns, the news waned. If it's not national news its old news and as bigger stories hit the news, Marc's began to fade. Eventually everyone forgot about him.

Everyone but me.

Chapter Thirty-Two

I DIDN'T HAVE MUCH TIME TO GO THROUGH MARC'S FILE AND KIRK had already warned me not to take it out of the building. So I did what self-respecting cop would do, I took out my cell, opened the camera app and took pictures of each page before Kirk caught me.

I'd look back through the photos tonight but right now I wanted to get home and see Mom and Pop Maybe I would have time to swing by Marge's house and do a little snooping.

I had just finished taking the last photo when Kirk returned with my report. "Here is your copy of the report for the insurance company and the rental car company."

"Thanks Kirk. I appreciate it."

Kirk motioned to the file in my hand, "You done with that?"

"Yes, I'm done." I handed Kirk the file.

"Anything stand out to you?"

"Not really. It's just as I expected. You said someone had opened the case a few years ago? I think I read her name in the file. This detective, Joy Sorenson, where is she now?"

Kirk frowned. "Sorenson. She didn't last long. She ended up leaving for a bigger department. Seattle, I think? I don't know."

"Do you have a contact number for her?"

"Not that I know of. Why do you want to talk to her? She didn't come up with anything."

"It was just an idea. I just thought it would be easier to talk to her in person is all."

"Are you investigating this? You know you're out of your jurisdiction, right? You don't have any authority here."

Kirk had that same weird angry look I had seen a few times before. He seemed to think I was here trying to step on his toes. "Kirk, a little professional courtesy wouldn't hurt, you know."

"What do you think I'm giving you now? I let you look at the file, didn't I? Don't go wearing out your welcome and causing a ruckus. You already got your windshield beat in. You want something else to happen?"

I stood up so fast my chair flew against the wall. "Did YOU break my windshield? Are you threatening me?"

Kirk looked genuinely surprised at my assumption. "What? No and I resent the fact that you would even suggest that. Look, I get it. Marc was your best friend and ghosts from our past can haunt us but stirring this up again will just cause you drama. Didn't you come here to get away from drama?"

"What would you know about it, Kirk?"

"Just because we are a little one horse town doesn't mean we don't keep up with the happenings of the world. I know all about your shooting. I read the headlines."

"Keeping up with my career, Kirk?"

"What kind of cop would I be if I didn't do a little research on the people coming into this town? I read all the news reports. Sounds like you had quite an incident. You're not just here to visit; you're escaping. Take my advice, Camden, we don't need your drama here."

I fashioned my face into as friendly a mask as I could muster. "Thanks for your help, Kirk. I really appreciate it." It wouldn't due to make Kirk my enemy or enter into a pissing contest with him. Kirk stared at me boldly; a smirk on his face. I wanted to wipe it off.

A woman's voice penetrated the silence in the room. "Kirk? Are you here?" A scuffling ensued followed by the woman's voice again. "You stop squirming right this minute!"

Kirk sighed, looked up at the ceiling and mouthed a silent prayer. To me he said, "My sister-in-law and nephew. I'll be right back."

Chapter Thirty-Three

WHILE KIRK WAS DEALING WITH THE COMMOTION OUT FRONT I WENT
into his office to grab the rental car receipts he had so conveniently
forgotten to give back to me. *Wait, my ass! I wasn't going to stick around
here any longer than I had too.*

I saw a large file cabinet behind Kirk's desk and a thought hit
me. I went to cabinet and found that the files were organized by the
year. I found the drawer for 1991, the year Marc went missing. I
opened it and glanced up and around. No cameras.

I quickly found the night in question and began to look at the
report listing all the calls for service. Everything was written down
on paper back then. No computers. I was actually glad that was the
case. It made it easier for me to snoop.

Back in 1991, the police department had utilized incident cards
that described all the calls for service each officer had responded to
during each shift. I started with eight p.m. the night Marc and I
went to the quarry and searched through to eight pm the next night.
In a 24- hour time period there wasn't too much exciting that had
happened

. . .

- 2130 - MISSING CAT on Orchard Street.

- 2230 - LOUD PARTY ON MORNINGVIEW – officers shut it down. Teenagers drinking. Three minors arrested.

- 2300 – dog barking on Serafina Drive. Baxter was taken inside by his owner.

- 2400 – Extra patrol on Sunset Ave. Mr. Gregory heard noises in his yard. Raccoons.

- 0600 - AUDIBLE ALARM. Store owner opening accidentally set it off.

- 1100 – Missing person. Mrs. Camden requested an officer investigate Mr. Forrester's claim his son was missing.

FROM THEN ON there was a flurry of calls of supposed sightings of Marc but none of them had case numbers associated. There were several calls missing person updates but I had already taken pictures of that file.

I took a quick snapshot of the calls for service log and shut the case file drawer.

"Whatcha doing?"

I whirled around. Caught! "Well if it isn't my favorite redhead."

Sarahbeth laughed and pranced over to me. "Imagine finding you here."

"And just what are YOU doing here, young lady?"

"I came down with my sister in law. Little Mikey is acting up again."

"What's the deal with your nephew anyway?"

"Remember my brother Sean?"

"Sure I do or at least I think I do. Sean was five years older than me so we weren't exactly friends growing up."

"Sean and Karen married straight out of high school and she got pregnant with Mikey right away. When Mikey was five, Sean was hired by a private contractor and went over seas. They needed the money. The base they were on got bombed and he didn't survive. Mikey took it especially hard. Seven years later Mikey gets to that difficult pre-teen stage and with no dad around he's been acting out. Kirk has really stepped up and tried to help but Karen is at her wits end."

I didn't mention that I had seen the shoplifting episode. "I'm sorry he's going through that. That must have been really hard on your whole family. Have you tried to work your magic on him with your art therapy?"

Sarahbeth smiled. "You remembered."

"Of course I remembered. You're hard to forget."

"I tried helping Mikey but I'm family so it doesn't have the same impact. Besides, Karen and Kirk wouldn't stop bugging me about what happened in our sessions and it's supposed to remain confidential. Mikey might be a little beyond my help at this point and I recommended a more traditional style of therapy."

Sarahbeth got a little teary eyed. "Sean's death was really hard on all of us. Mom and dad have never been the same."

I wanted to hug her and comfort her but in a flash she shook off her melancholy and with a mischievous grin she asked, "You wanna get out of here?"

I almost exhaled in relief. "Yes please!"

"Let's go out the back," she giggled. "I don't feel like dealing with my family any further today!"

NEITHER DID I.

Chapter Thirty-Four

I FOLLOWED SARAHBETH OUT OF THE POLICE STATION BACK DOOR and into the blinding sunlight. It was nearing noon and the sun had gotten warmer. Harmony didn't usually have hot days in the town but today was shaping up to be a warm one.

Sarahbeth fanned herself, "Wow it's getting hot. Want to go swimming?"

"I thought you had mural painting to do today?"

"I do what I want. That's the luxury of being your own boss. So what do you say? Want to go for a dip?"

"Sure."

Sarahbeth motioned toward her car. "I'll drive. We can swing by your place on the way and grab you something to wear and some towels."

When we reached my house, Sarahbeth stayed in the car while I ran up the front steps. Mom was in the kitchen making lunch. "Hi son. What are you up to? Are you hungry? I'm making your dad some lunch. Would you like a sandwich?"

I kissed ma on the cheek. "Can't stay. I'm going swimming with a friend."

She raised an eyebrow but didn't pry. "Then how about I make a couple sandwiches that you can take with you?"

"Mom, have I ever told you that you're my favorite parent? How was church?"

"It was good. Pastor Simon preached on forgiveness." A snuck a peak at me from the corner of her eye and I raised an eyebrow her way. She continued, "Mr. Forrester was there. He said he ran into you last night. He seemed very sad and was extremely apologetic. He said to tell you he was sorry for getting out of line."

"Why didn't he stop by to apologize himself?"

"Now Jason, that man has had some terrible grief. Be a little more gracious."

"Mom, when we were kids he accused me of having something to do with Marc's disappearance. He was always a cruel man to him. He never apologized. Fourteen years later he still acts like a jerk and still can't say he's sorry?"

"Some people have a hard time admitting when they are wrong."

"I'm glad you can forgive him, Ma, but I don't think I can. Not yet."

"Can you forgive yourself?"

My breath caught. "What do you mean?"

Mom turned away from the counter and the sandwiches to give me her full attention. "I mean, you seem to have a heavy burden on your shoulders, son."

"Dad told you?"

"You think he keeps anything from me? Besides I keep up with you just fine on my own."

"Geez, for a small town, people here sure are good at keeping tabs on someone three thousand miles away."

Mom swatted me with her dishtowel. "You're my son. You never come home to visit. So I did what any mother would do, I set a Google alert."

I laughed. "What do you know about Google alerts?"

"Sharon down at the library showed me how to do it. When

your name hits the news, I know about it; since you don't tell me stuff."

"Mom, you don't need to hear about my working environment. It's ugly and nothing happy happens."

"I can handle more than you think I can, son. So, what I want to know is, can you forgive yourself for shooting that man?"

"There's nothing to forgive. He was burglarizing the place, hit the owner over the head with a pipe and when I tried to arrest him he grabbed for a gun. It was him or me."

"I understand you were doing your job. That doesn't mean it doesn't get to you. Taking the life of another human is a heavy thing." Mom reached over and laid her hand on my face. "I know you. You don't just brush things off and if its weighing on you, you need to forgive yourself."

I grabbed her hand and held it in both of mine. "I know, Ma. I'm fine, I promise. I can forgive myself just fine."

"Then why can't you forgive Mr. Forrester? He didn't hurt you. He didn't hurt Marc. The only thing that man is guilty of is letting his grief get the best of him. You think he drinks because he's happy?"

"No, I guess not."

"Then show the man the grace you would afford yourself; that your GOING to afford yourself and be kind."

"Yes ma'am."

Mom hugged me and handed me a brown paper bag with sand-wiches. "I threw in a couple of fresh baked cookies. Now go have fun with that young lady and be respectful."

"How'd you know I was going with a young lady?"

"I told you – Google!"

I tried to hide my smile. "You're a sage, Ma." I wet to my room, changed into my swimming trunks, grabbed two towels and ran out the door. "I'll be home for dinner!" I yelled as I jumped down the porch steps, just like I was fourteen again.

Chapter Thirty-Five

SARAHBETH POINTED HER LITTLE RED CAR DOWN THE FAMILIAR DIRT road and we sped toward the quarry. We drove past the gated off section where we used to jump and she glanced at me with interest as I watched it go by.

"No jumping," she said with a small smile. We turned into a turnout about half a mile away from the jumping spot and parked. We grabbed our things and went down to the beach area. I say beach but really it was like gravel.

In California we had real beaches. Soft sand with waves that made your toes curl. Here it was rocky lake inlets and "sand" was more like pebbles.

We found a spot clear of brush and laid out our towels. Before I could even sit down, Sarahbeth had stripped to her bathing suit. The lyrics "Itsy-bitsy-teeny-weeny-yellow-polka-dot-bikini" instantly ran through what was left of my mind and I admired her as she picked her way towards the water. No wading in; she just dove head first under the cold water.

I quickly stripped to my shorts and followed suit. The water was so cold. The icy runoff from the Rocky Mountains never warmed up. It was bracing but I felt myself come alive in a way I hadn't in years. Between the nostalgia of being home and the tumultuousness of the last few days, I knew I needed this.

Sarahbeth swam over to me and dunked me under the water. When I came up for air she was already yards away and swimming towards the floating dock out on the water. I shook the water from my ears and took off after her. My strong smooth strokes warmed up my muscles. By the time I reached the float, Sarahbeth had already hoisted herself up and was stretched out soaking up the afternoon rays. I plopped down next to her and we lay there in comfortable silence soaking up the vitamin D and quiet.

"So what the big city like?"

"Roland isn't really that big but its definitely a city. It certainly isn't as quiet as Harmony."

"I'd love to visit some day."

"No you wouldn't. It's a ghetto."

"We could always go sight seeing. You live near San Francisco, right?"

"Yes, I am. There's a lot to to see. California is a big state." I ventured into her daydream. "We could go see the Golden Gate Bridge and there's so still a multitude of museums I have yet to visit. There's much more to California than beaches and San Francisco though."

"So maybe you should educate me." She rolled over and squinted at me. "Seriously, I should go home with you."

I glanced over at her. "You trying to get out of here?"

"I'd run away with you, Jason."

"I'm not looking to run away and it wouldn't be 'away' it would just be home for me."

Sarahbeth smiled, "So take me home with you."

"Sweetie, I'd like nothing more than to have you along for the ride but....are you sure you want to leave all this?" I gestured towards the open water and wide sky.

She flopped onto her back in a mock huff. "All of what; this small town that smells like cow manure, the family trauma? I want to SEE things. I want to BE places. I want to experience MORE. I won't get that if I stay here."

"You have a college education. You could go anywhere."

"That's what I mean. I'd just rather go with you. Take me with you?"

"Let's just enjoy today, shall we?"

"Why? Is there someone back home?"

"No. It's not that."

"I bet there is. What is she, your partner or something?"

My mind flashed to Lizzie. I had never really thought of her as more than my friend. If I was honest enough I would say I missed her and I was having a harder time away from her than I thought I would. "I do have a partner and she is a female but she's just a friend."

"What's her name?"

"Lizzie."

Sarahbeth spit her name out. "Lizzie. Sounds like a priss."

I found myself a little on the defense. "She's not a priss. In fact she's been through a lot. She's tougher than most men I know."

"I thought all female cops were lesbians."

"You have a little mean streak in you don't you?"

"I was just stating a fact. Don't go getting your panties in a twist over it."

"See if you came home with me you'd be on the other side of police work. It's not good for married folks."

"Who said anything about being married? I'm good with living in sin."

"If you can't handle your jealousy now, all these miles away, you certainly couldn't handle it there."

Sarahbeth's voice became stony. "You're probably right."

I looked at her and hoped I hadn't just ruined a nice afternoon. "Don't you have a boyfriend here? I can't imagine you being single. Guys must be lining up to spend time with you."

"Oh they are. I just happen to prefer the sullen silent types who only come around for a week at a time."

I reached out and grabbed her hand and held it softly. Two seconds later Sarahbeth pulled her hand away, got up and without a word dove back into the water. I watched her swim towards the shore with just a tingle of regret.

Halfway to shore, Sarahbeth stopped and tread water. She yelled, "Are you coming or not? Those cookies aren't going to eat themselves."

I closed my eyes and soaked in a few more rays. I sighed out loud as I thought about the cold lake water in my immediate future, got up and dove in after her.

By the time I reached the shore, Sarahbeth had made a nice little picnic for us. We spent the next few hours napping in the sun, eating and swimming. The tension between us seemed to have been forgotten, for the moment.

Chapter Thirty-Six

As Sarahbeth drove us back into town, I asked her to do me a favor. "Can we stop by Marge Freelander's house?"

"That old crank? Why?"

I wasn't sure I wanted Sarahbeth to know I was following a hunch so I avoided her question. "She still lives in the same place, doesn't she?"

"Yes. That old biddy will die in that house. Tell me what you're up to."

"Only if you promise not to make a huge deal out of it…and you don't tell Kirk."

Sarahbeth's face clouded with suspicion. "I promise."

"The night Marc disappeared, Marge heard a loud argument coming from their house. She swore it was Marc and his dad."

"So what?"

"The police looked into it but the timeline doesn't fit and she was dismissed. I just thought I'd stop and see if she has anything else she might remember."

"You're really digging into this aren't you?"

"No, not really. I just figured a conversation couldn't hurt."

. . .

FIVE MINUTES later and Sarahbeth pulled up to Marge's ancient house. I could see Marge, busy in her front garden, tending to her flowers and spying on everyone who walked by. She stood up, held a hand to shade her eyes and squinted at the sight of our car.

I got out and stepped onto the sidewalk. Sarahbeth started to open her car door but I instructed her, "Stay here."

I walked to the white picket fence separating the sidewalk from Marge's domain. "Marge Freelander?"

The elderly Marge didn't budge from her lower beds. "Who's asking?"

"My name is Jason Camden."

Marge dropped her spade and ambled over to meet me at the fence. "You're that Camden boy. Your dad owns the hardware shop over on Main Street."

"Yes ma'am."

"What can I do for you son?"

I shifted back and forth, suddenly nervous about pestering her. "I don't know if you remember my friend Marc Forrester? He used to live next door to you?"

Marge's voice became soft and her face took on a sadness that encouraged me to pry. "I remember Marc very well. They never did find him, you know."

"I know."

"What is it you want to know?"

"You told the cops that you heard arguing that night?"

"Yep. Lots of yelling coming from that place over there."

I cleared my throat. "You told the officer that you heard the arguing at eleven that night. How certain are you about the time?"

"I'm definite about the time. The yelling was so loud it woke me and I looked at the clock."

"What exactly did you hear?"

"Well, I couldn't hear what they were saying exactly. I just heard two men yelling and glass breaking."

"At eleven p.m.?"

"Yes."

I looked over at Mark's house and tried to imagine an argument so loud that it woke this little old lady. "I don't know if the police told you or not but that night, Marc and I had gone swimming at the quarry. He left my house at eleven. Are you sure it was Mark and his dad that you heard?"

"I don't know who was arguing. All I know is that there was a ruckus loud enough to wake the dead. That man was a horrid drunk and he was always yelling at that poor kid."

"Mr. Forrester?"

Marge leaned heavily on the fence between us. "I've known that man since he was a boy. He used to be so happy. I watched him grow up! When he met his pretty little wife he was over the moon. They were so excited about having a baby. She was really the sweetest thing I'd ever met, that wife of his." Marge shook her head. "Terrible tragedy when she died." Marge sighed, "I suppose a sadness like that is bound to change a man."

"How did he change?"

"He started drinking. Neglected that boy something awful. I used to babysit him you know?"

I turned at the sound of a car door opening. Sarahbeth must've gotten antsy in the car. She stepped up to the curb next to me.

Marge squinted at Sarahbeth. "And who's this?"

Sarahbeth held out her hand, "Hi, I'm Sarahbeth Johnson."

Marge examined Sarahbeth over the rim of her glasses. She looked skeptical but small town manners demanded she shake her hand. "I know who you are. Your Kirk's littlest sister, aren't you?"

"Yes ma'am."

"The girl who likes to paint pictures all over our historical buildings."

Sarahbeth stuck out her chin. "It's just one mural and it was approved by the mayor!"

"It's an eyesore, young lady!"

I interrupted before this conversation could get out of hand. "Marge, can I ask, did you ever see Marc with any bruises or anything?"

She seemed offended by the question. "You mean like child

abuse? No way. His dad may have been a very troubled man but I don't think he would ever lay a hand on that boy."

"What do you think happened to Mark?"

"I told the officers everything I know."

Sarahbeth asked, "What about rumors?"

"Oh sure. There were rumors that he ran off on his own. There were rumors he got kidnapped." Marge looked at down at her hands and pretended to wipe dirt off them. "If I remember correctly there were rumors that your little boyfriend here had a little something to do with his disappearance. Rumors that Marc drowned out there in the quarry and you came home without him."

Sarahbeth pushed the fence angrily, "That's not true!"

I quieted Sarahbeth with a hand on her shoulder. "Yes ma'am, I remember those rumors all too vividly."

Marge looked me in the eye. "Well then you know rumors are just that and can't be trusted. Although, usually there's a bit of truth to them."

I straightened my back. "Not in that one." Marge and I eyed each other for a brief second. I decided it was time to go. Marge hadn't provided any useful information and I was starting to get uncomfortable. I thanked Marge for her time. I could feel Marge's eyes on our backs as Sarahbeth and I walked to her car.

I opened the driver door for Sarahbeth and before she got in she laid a hand on my chest. "That old lady is just a nosy gossip. I don't think she heard anything that night. I think she just wanted the attention."

I kissed Sarahbeth on the nose. "Come on, let's go."

I closed the door and walked around to the passenger door. I was about to get in when Marge called out to me. "You try that cop?"

I paused. "What cop?"

"That lady cop that reopened the case. Joy something or other. She came around to talk to me just like you're doing, only she seemed to think she had a lead. It seemed she knew a little something."

"You wouldn't happen to have her number, would you?"

"Somewhere. If I find her card I'll swing by your dads shop and give it to him."

I waved my thanks to Marge and got in the car. Sarahbeth stepped on the gas and I scolded her a little. "I appreciate you trying to defend me but you didn't have to get all fired up like that. She's just an old lady."

"Yeah well this town is full of nosey old bitches. Someone should put her in her place."

"Are you mad because she said I had been the subject of nasty rumor or are you angry about her making noise over your mural?"

"You know that old lady called an actual town meeting to try and get them to make me stop? Called it graffiti!"

I laughed. "That explains it."

"It's not funny, Jason!"

It was clear Sarahbeth was no longer in a fun mood. We drove in silence and when we reached my house I barely had time to get out before she angrily peeled out of my driveway.

REDHEADS!

Chapter Thirty-Seven

MONDAY MORNING ARRIVED IN ITS USUAL FASHION, TOO SOON. I needed to venture back to the car rental place and trade in my damaged truck for another.

My paperwork in hand, I jogged down to the café where I had left my truck yesterday morning. Thank goodness Kirk hadn't been irritated with me enough to tow it.

It was a slow, tortuous drive back to the airport but I made it without hitting anything or swerving off into a ditch. I went to the rental desk and explained what had happened. I handed over my copy of the police report along with a lengthy apology. After filling the paperwork for another vehicle, this time a small, reasonably less expensive, compact, I went outside to wait.

It seemed no one was in a hurry to bring me another chance to bankrupt them, so while I waited, I went through the pictures of the case file I had taken with my phone. Nothing jumped out at me.

I wondered if about the party call and the subsequent arrest of the juveniles involved. Maybe one of those drunk teens had seen something and not realized its significance? The incident had occurred around the right time of night. Drunk teenagers aren't exactly the most credible witnesses but it was worth a shot. If I could find them. I read the names of those arrested. *Well, well, well. I know you.* I recognized one of these characters and knew just where I was going next. If they ever brought me my car!

Eventually a young man in his twenties drove up with my new rental car and handed me the keys. "Here you are, sir. Sorry you had to deal with that."

This was a first! This guy was actually apologizing. To me! If this had been California I'd be having to explain myself repeatedly as well as pay through the nose for the repairs. If they gave me another car at all.

I got my car and drove straight back to Bojangles. Shelly was busing bustling food back and forth between tables and when I asked for Ben she said whirled past me with a quick "Ben's not here!"

I decided I would wait until the crowd had thinned a bit and ordered a piece of pie that I ate while I read the local newspaper. I was engrossed in an article touting the towns excitement over the upcoming Fourth of July carnival when Shelly fell, exhausted, into the chair across from me.

I shoveled another bite of pie into my mouth before rudely mumbling, "I didn't realize you guys got so busy!"

"When Ben is gone I run like my hair is on fire!"

"Where is he?"

"Once a week Ben drives to Deertail and buys all of our meat at the butchers there. It's better than the frozen meat we could buy from the distributer and to be honest, I think he likes to get out of here for an afternoon."

"When will he be back?"

Shelly glanced at her watch and then rubbed her tired eyes with her hands. "Whew, only a few more hours. He is usually back by six or seven at the latest." Shelly got up and tightened her apron strings. She grabbed my empty pie plate. "If you want coffee, you are going to have to be a gentleman and get it yourself." She smiled before twirling away, back to her hungry customers.

I took Shelly's advice and found the coffeepot and a to-go Styrofoam cup. Before I left, I tucked a twenty under the register.

I drove the few blocks to Camden Hardware and went in to see my dad. The front bell jingled and Dad looked up from his stack of receipts he was sorting. "Son, I'm glad you're here." He set down his papers and reached into his shirt pocket, withdrawing a small business card. "Marge stopped by and left this for you."

I examined the card.

Officer Joy Sullivan

Harmony Police Department.

The Harmony Police Department part had been scratched out and a phone number had been written in pen underneath it. It wasn't a local number.

"Thanks, Pop." I took the card outside to the front walk and pulled out my cell phone. I dialed the number handwritten on the card but was disappointed when I reached a voicemail. "Hello. You have reached the voicemail of Lieutenant Joy Sullivan of the Portland Police Department. Please, leave me a message and I'll get back to you as soon as I can." *Beeeeep.*

I left a short message explaining who I was and asking her to call me back. With Dad's nose stuck in his paperwork and nothing better to do at the moment, I went to the library and checked in with Ma. Maybe I was a hoping, just a little, that I'd run into Katie graffitiing the walls of the institution.

I walked into the cool library and had to squint in the dim lighting. I found my mom in the science fiction section, shoving paperbacks into their Dewey Decimal assigned spaces. Mom looked up in surprise. "Well what in the heck are you doing here?"

"I thought I would stop in and say hi to my favorite librarian. Make sure she wasn't googling anything inappropriate."

Mom slapped my arm playfully. "While you are here, why don't you grab yourself something to read, son."

I grimaced. "I'm on vacation. I don't want to work."

"Here. Check out this book." Mom handed me a small paperback with a robot on the front. "There's enough fantasy in that book that you will forget all about work, and girls…" She widened her eyes at me, "…and get lost in a vacation on Mars."

I growled in mock annoyance as I took the book from her outstretched hand. "Yes ma'am."

Mom went back to stuffing book shelves and I meandered around for a moment, pretending to look at the spines of the so-called vacation fodder. Sarahbeth was nowhere to be found but I did want to check out her mural. I walked outside and found her artwork displayed on the west side of the building. I looked it over in admiration. She was quite good. The mural depicted a large scene of a small town that I assumed was Harmony. Kids played and the American flag flew high above them all.

There really wasn't anything to do right now. Ben was gone for the next few hours, Sarahbeth was evading me, both my folks were busy working and, I checked my cell phone, Joy Sullivan still hadn't called me back.

There was only one thing left to do. I retrieved my car, drove home, took my book out to the backyard and climbed into my dad's hammock.

The gentle sway of the hammock, the smell of pine and the warmth of the shaded sun lulled me. The story of Martians and soldiers at war put me right to sleep.

I dreamt of Marc. We were fourteen again and back at the quarry. I watched as Marc laughed, ran and jumped off the cliff. The moon was huge and Marc made a small shadow against it before he droppedto water below. I waited for the splash but it didn't come.

I went to the edge of the jumping cliff and looked down towards the water. Marc was gone. The water didn't even ripple. It was smooth as glass. I was alone.

I screamed his name over and over. I scrambled down the rocks to the shore below, sure I would find his body broken and lifeless. Marc wasn't there either. I scrambled back to where we had dropped our bikes and found only my own. Marc's was gone.

Had he played a trick on me? Was he hiding? And then a frightening thought roared into my head; Had he ever been with me? Did I really come here alone and imagine the rest?

My dream shifted and now dark rolling fog shut out the moon

and I was enveloped in darkness. I walked my bike back along the road and saw a shining light up ahead. It was coming fast, like a train. The light got larger and larger and so bright that I threw my arm across my eyes. Suddenly the light morphed into the beam of a flashlight. An adult Kirk in uniform stood before me. He was telling me I was guilty. That Marc was dead. That he had burned in a fire.

I tried to scream at Kirk, to tell him he was wrong. I tried to tell him that Marc had gone into the water but I couldn't find him. I opened my mouth and tried to yell but no sound came out. Instead, my mouth and lungs started to fill with smoke. My lungs started burning! Burning. Burning. Smoke everywhere!

I awoke with a start and gasped for air. What the hell was that about? This dreaming thing was getting out of hand. I couldn't shake that feeling you get when you have a nightmare. The feeling that everything that happened in the dream was still there, just out of reach, maybe just on the other side of some weird alternate universe. Damn Ma and her science fiction.

The smell of smoke lingered in my nostrils. I toed the ground and set the hammock to a gentle swing. I tried to reclaim my earlier calmness as I wondered what the dream could have meant. My efforts were almost immediately broken by the screams of a fire engine and I realized that the smell of smoke had gotten stronger. This was not in my head.

I jumped up and ran to the front of the house just in time to see the fire truck pulling up.

You have GOT to be kidding me!

My rental car was fully engulfed in flames and putrid black smoke.

What the hell!!! I felt like a total tool just standing there, watching helplessly as the Harmony Fire Department doused the sloppy mess. The acrid smell of burning rubber and the heat causing the windows to pop was so out of the ordinary that all of the neighbors, who were home, came out to watch.

As the flames diminished and dirty soot water ran in a stream through the neighborhood gutter, one of the firefighters approached. "Is this your car, sir?"

"It's a rental. I just got it today."

He took of his helmet and scratched his head. "Hate to say it but it's completely totaled."

"Any idea how the fire could've started?"

The firefighter tucked his helmet under his arm and gazed appreciatively at the now extinguished pile of blackened metal. "Ignition source could be electrical but it looks more like arson."

"What? Arson? You mean someone did this on purpose?"

"I'm afraid so. Someone tossed something inside of it and it caught on fire. Maybe a rag or a lit match…I'll know more after I examine it further."

I groaned out loud. "UGH!"

"You have any enemies?"

"I wish I knew! My last rental car had the windshield busted out."

"Looks like someone is trying to send you a message, son."

"I don't even live here." I gestured at the house behind me. "I'm just here visiting my folks."

"Could it be someone has something against your folks?"

"Do you even know my folks? My dad is John Camden."

The firefighter broke into a grin. "Hey, I know him! He is always so helpful when I go into the hardware store. Your dad is good people. I can't imagine anyone having anything against him." He put his hat back on. "Must be you then, kid. Here comes Kirk, maybe he can help you out."

"Gee thanks," I said to his retreating figure.

Kirk let out a whistle as joined me on the lawn. "Well I'll be damned, Camden. Who did you piss off this time?"

"Kirk I didn't do anything to anyone. Someone lit my car on fire and I want to know what you're going to do about it?"

"What would you LIKE me to do about it, big shot cop? It's not like I can lift any prints." Kirk smiled, "that thing is toast!" He turned me in feigned seriousness. "Is it possible that you did this on accident? You take up smoking recently?"

"Cut the shit, Kirk. Someone seems to have taking a liking to vandalizing my cars and I'm worried about what they are going to do next."

Kirk scratched his chin as if he was seriously pondering my predicament. "That does seem to be a problem, doesn't it." He shifted gears. "Here you go." Kirk handed me a piece of paper with a case number on it. "This here is the report number for the report I'll be writing up. Report should be available within ten working days. You're going to need a copy for the car rental agency of course."

"Thanks for nothing."

Kirk ignored my remark. "I'll order a tow truck to get this thing out of here within the hours." Kirk tipped his stupid hat at me and walked towards the car. He was halfway across the front lawn when he slowly spun back around. "Say, Jason. I heard you were over at Marge Freelander's house yesterday."

The hair on the back of my neck stood at attention. "Yeah. So what?"

"What were you doing over there?"

"Putting my mind at ease."

"Well, I heard you were asking about Marc. You find out anything useful?"

"Not a thing."

Kirk tipped his big ridiculous hat at me once again. "Well ok then."

I watched as Kirk drove slowly down the block. I was beginning to think he might do anything to keep me from looking into Mark's disappearance any further.

Maybe, just maybe he wasn't the only one.

Chapter Thirty-Eight

THE LOCAL TOW COMPANY CAME AND HAULED THE BURNED OUT CAR away. I washed down the street where the fireball had left char marks. I wanted to get it as clean as possible before mom or Dad came home and got too worried.

Once I had cleaned up the majority of the mess, I jumped in the shower and tried to wash the scent of burning rubber out of my hair and nose. I shut off the water but took my time getting out. The buildup of steam in the tiny bathroom felt like a warm cocoon that I wasn't entirely in a hurry to leave. I heard my cell phone ringing from my room. I quickly wrapped a towel around myself, ran down the hall to my room and grabbed the phone. "Hello?"

A female voice said, "Yes. This is Joy Sullivan, returning a call from Jason Camden?"

"This is Jason Camden. Thank you for calling me back Lieutenant. I used to live in Harmony, Montana and its my understanding that you were a police sergeant there at one time?"

"That's correct."

"Do you remember opening a missing person cold case? The victim was Marc Forrester."

"How could I forget?"

"It was that memorable?"

"The kid went missing with zero clues. That is pretty unusual."

"Did you ever come up with anything? Any clues that the original investigation might not have discovered?"

"Not particularly but I didn't get very far before I was shut down."

"Shut down by whom?"

"The police chief. He told me to stop. He said I was upsetting people by investigating it. I really think the only person I was upsetting was Kirk Johnson though. That guy was so jealous and he was worried I might outshine him. He was an asshole. Is he still working there?"

"Unfortunately."

Joy continued, "I already had my application submitted here when shit started happening. I was done. I gave up. I didn't push the issue because I was on my way out."

"What kind of shit started happening?"

"Silly stuff. Incidents happened that, when considered by themselves, were completely insignificant. The doorbell ringing but when I answered; no one would be there. Flat tires, dead birds on the front porch, juvenile stuff."

"Do you think It was kids?"

"Nope. I think someone was trying to rattle me. Even though they were juvenile attempts and nothing really harmful I truly believe it stemmed from my interest in Marc Forrester's case."

"I've been in town a few days and I have been looking in to Mark's case as well. I've had a few weird things happen to me too. In fact, today, someone lit my car on fire."

"Damn! I would watch your back if I was you."

"Getting back to your investigation. Did you have any suspicions about what had happened to Mark?"

"On the night Mark went missing, there was a party. I talked to several of the kids that were arrested and one kinda stood out. Ben something? I can't remember his last name off the top of my head."

"That's ok, I know who you mean."

"He wasn't too happy about answering my questions. One of

the other two arrested, said he thought he saw Mark riding his bike on the way home."

"Which kid?"

I can't remember his name. I interviewed both him and Ben simultaneously, and rather casually, and that Ben kid shut his friend up pretty quickly."

"That sounds pretty suspicious."

"I thought it was odd to say the least."

I think I had all the information I was going toget from Lt. Sullivan. "Thank you for calling me, LT."

"Anything else I can do for you?"

"Not now. Can I call you again if I need to?"

"Of course. Say, aren't you a cop somewhere in California?"

"How'd you know?"

"I get the news here in Portland."

"Enough said." I exhaled in frustration. "Seems like we can't keep anything private anymore."

"Don't sweat it, kid. Sounds like a good shoot."

"It was. They put me on the beach until the investigation is over but I know it'll turn out in my favor."

"Take it from someone who's been there a time or two. You're not doing your job if someone isn't complaining. Enjoy the respite while you can. The job will be there when you get back."

"IF I go back."

Sullivan laughed, "Portland is hiring!"

"I'm good. Thanks."

"If you ever get tired of the bullshit out there in California, you just let me know. We don't treat our cops like criminals here."

I ended the call and sat there for a minute, reflecting on what Joy Sullivan had told me. Ben? Could Ben know something he hadn't told me?

I had to talk to him. I checked the clock on my cell phone. Six p.m. Maybe he would be back from Deertail by now.

I dressed quickly but instead of heading out I went to the kitchen and began making dinner. My folks would be home form work soon and I knew Mom would appreciate this. Besides, I needed to think about how I was going to approach Ben.

I usually had others to bounce ideas off of and briefly while I cooked I considered calling Lizzie. I picked up the phone to call her but immediately put it down again. I had mixed feelings about being so close to Lizzie.

Sarahbeth's comments had eaten their way into my brain and caused me to question myself. Did I have feelings for Lizzie? She was someone special for sure. Sam was definitely as awesome as kids could come.

Lizzie was my partner. We worked together. Who successfully mixes work and pleasure? No one. Its true that cops frequently dated co-workers but I wasn't sure I wanted to take a chance on making our relationship a personal one; at least not any more personal than it already was. Besides I had no indication that Lizzie would even be interested in me.

And what about Sarahbeth? She was talented, beautiful and I really liked her but could we really have anything beyond a brief little fling while I was home? I smiled to myself. Sarahbeth was pretty temperamental.

I was leaving in a few days anyway. After everything that had occurred, I was actually looking forward to getting out of here. Being home wasn't very relaxing now that someone was making it difficult.

Someone was going to a lot of trouble to make me uncomfortable and throw me off Marc's case. Well, they didn't know me that well. I don't give up and my cop sense was telling me not to leave here without finding out once and for all what had happened that night.

I owed it to Marc and I owed it to myself to put this to rest once and for all.

Chapter Thirty-Nine

Mom and Dad came home and we enjoyed a leisurely dinner. I made sure not to mention the car fire or my phone call with Lieutenant Sullivan. When we had finished, I sent my folks to the living room to enjoy their nightly dose of jeopardy while I washed up.

Once I had dried and stowed the last dish, I knew I couldn't put it off any longer. I needed to talk to Ben. I no longer had a car so I changed into my running clothes and slipped on my running shoes.

"Ma? Pop? I'm heading out for a run." I called out as I stepped out onto the front porch. It was still warm but I needed the exercise and the run would give me time to formulate what I was going to say to Ben. I started off slowly and when my muscled had warmed up I let my legs go full stride.

Chapter Forty

FIFTEEN MINUTES LATER, I MADE MY WAY INSIDE BOJANGLES CAFÉ. I didn't see Shelly even though the tables were almost vacant.

I brazenly ventured through the kitchen doors were I found Ben cleaning the grill. He looked up with surprise, "Hey man what's up?"

"Just out for a run and thought I'd stop by."

"Shell said you were in earlier. Sorry I wasn't here. I had to go out of town to pick up the meat. Want a hamburger? It's fresh and the grill is cleaned."

"No thanks." I patted my stomach. "I just had dinner with my folks."

Ben smiled knowingly. "How about a beer then?"

"That sounds like heaven, thanks."

Ben popped the cap off an ice-cold beer and handed it to me. I leaned against the sink watching Ben prep condiments for the next day.

He must've felt me staring at him. Humans are predictable. It is very rare that they can stay silent. They need talking. Police Interview 101, the longer the interviewer stays silent, the more restless the suspect becomes. If an interviewer can stay silent long enough, the suspect will just start talking to fill the silence. Inevitably he or she starts spilling their guts because they just cant stand the silence. As if on cue Ben starts the conversation. "What's new, man?"

"There was a fire out at my house today."

Ben barely blinked. "Everyone ok? No one was hurt were they?"

"Someone set my rental car on fire. No one was hurt."

Ben stopped slicing vegetables long enough to express concern. I wasn't sure if he was faking it or not. "Someone set your car on fire?"

"Yep."

Ben laughed as he returned to his prep work. "Man, who did you piss off?"

"That's just it, as far as I know I haven't pissed anyone off." I paused before saying what I was thinking. "I think whoever is bothering me is doing it because I was nosing around about Marc's missing person case."

Ben didn't break stride. He threw a handful of potatoes into the deep fryer, flipped a burger on the freshly cleaned grill and chopped mushrooms to throw down next to it. "What about Marc's case?"

"I've been kinda nosing around. I looked at the original file."

"Kirk actually let you into his precious police house and let you poke around like that?"

"Yes and no."

Ben threw a piece of cheese on top of the softening mushrooms. I wont lie; despite having just eaten my mouth was starting to water. I pushed aside thoughts of the delicious mushroom cheeseburger. "I found the list of calls for service that night. I figured that maybe there would be other calls for service in the area. Turns out there were a few things that happened that night."

"Like what?"

"For one thing, Marge Freelander heard arguing but that was at eleven. I know it couldn't have been Marc and his dad because Marc was on his way home from my house at eleven.

"Ok, so who was doing the arguing?"

"I'm not sure. I'm not even sure Marge heard what she thinks she heard."

"You think she was making it up? Like for attention or something?"

"No. I think what she heard was real but I'm still working on the theory that the people arguing were not Marc and his dad."

"What does that theory have to do someone burning your car to ground?"

"Hear me out. There was also a party that night." I dropped that little nugget and watched Ben for a reaction. So far he was holding it together. Maybe Joy had been wrong. Maybe Ben had zero to do with this. I pressed the issue. "There was a party that night and the cops busted it up. They said kids were drinking and a fight broke out. Some of the kids got arrested. The report said you were one of those kids."

"I remember that. Jordan Thompson, JT's older brother, had a party and it was pretty fun. I remember the cops breaking it up and getting hauled in but I don't remember there being any fight."

"How did the cops find out about the party in the first place?"

"I have no idea. We were probably being too loud and some neighbor called or something. Man, you know how it was back then. We all got a little crazy."

"I was fourteen and a total geek. I wasn't really getting crazy back then."

"Well I was sixteen and let me tell you, between the booze and the girls and maybe a little weed now and then, we were crazy."

"There were girls at the party?"

Ben laughed out loud at my question. "Of course there were! What's a party without girls?"

"Was Shelly there?"

"No she wasn't hanging out with us back then."

"I didn't see Jordan Thompson's name on the arrest report."

"He wasn't there. What I mean by that is that Jordan was out on a beer run while we were getting busted." Ben looked like he had had enough of my questions. "Look man. What does all of this have to do with Marc going missing?"

I lied. "I think that maybe Marc's dad DID have something to do with Marc's disappearance but I just don't know how. I was hoping maybe someone saw Marc on his way home. If someone saw him after he left my house then…"

Ben interrupted me. "…they also wouldn't think you had something to do with it right? Clear your own name?"

"Screw you. I was never a suspect. Marc was the closest thing to a brother I have ever had!"

Ben could see he had struck the right nerve and was happy to keep dancing on it. "I'm just saying…we were kids. If something happened out there at the quarry, if Marc got hurt and you couldn't help him, if someone took him and you were too scared to tell, no one would be mad at that. You were just a kid."

Police Interviewing 101, don't let the suspect push your buttons and DON'T lose your temper. Failed!

I stormed out of the kitchen. *Screw him. Shit. Why did I let him throw me off track like that?* I went outside into the darkness. I paced the sidewalk in the light of Bojangles dancing boot, trying to get myself under control.

The weather had turned cold and I looked up at the moonless sky. It almost looked like rain. I heard rolling thunder in the distance and smelled rain in the air even though not a drop had fallen yet. How the hell could a storm come in so quickly?

I slammed an angry fist against the side of the cafe. *Pull it together Camden.* Ben had clearly been trying to distract me from questioning him further and I had just given him what he wanted. I had let my own guilt and anger get the best of my judgement and now I would never get answers from Ben. Not the ones I was looking for. *No. I wasn't going to let this happen.*

The first raindrops started to fall as I stormed back into the restaurant. I went to the swinging door and pushed it open, hard. Ben was gone. I walked slowly through the kitchen to the office door. It was slightly ajar and Ben was talking to someone on the phone.

"He's asking around. Doing too much looking. I was able to hold him off for the night but I don't think we can stop him asking questions for good. Maybe we should just tell him?"

Who was Ben talking to? Tell me what?

There was a few seconds of silence and then. "Look man, I.... yeah I know but... fine!" Ben slammed down the phone.

I was about to enter the office and confront him when I heard a female voice in the room with Ben. "Ben, just tell Jason what happened. Put his mind to rest once and for all." *Shelly.*

"Are you kidding? He's a cop Shell. You don't really think he's gonna understand do you? If Jason learns the truth you think he won't go blabbing?"

"But you didn't do anything wrong!"

"Shell, lying by omission is the same as lying outright. I might as well be guilty. You know someone's been stalking Jason? Set his car on fire, busted out his windshield!"

"What? Who?"

"Who do you think?" Ben continued, "I'm going over there tonight. We will figure out the best way to handle this."

"Ben don't. Don't go over there."

"Maybe he will listen to reason?"

"When has he EVER listened to reason?"

I had heard enough. My stomach churned and I felt like I was going to vomit. I quietly made my way back outside the café. *Ben and Shelly. They knew. They knew what had happened to Marc and had said nothing!* My head was spinning. *Who had Ben been talking to on the phone? Whoever that person was, Ben was meeting him tonight. Maybe if I follow him I could figure out who this someone was.*

My mind was made up and as if the universe sensed the impending deluge of discovered secrets, the heavens opened and it started to pour.

Chapter Forty-One

I HAD ONE PROBLEM. I HAD NO CAR. OK TWO PROBLEMS, NO CAR AND it was pouring. The restaurant would be closing in about fifteen minutes and I had to find a way to follow Ben when he left. I didn't have time to run home and get Pop's car. I had left my cell phone at home. I really only had one choice.

I ran to the last known remaining payphone in the United States. It was two blocks from the café, located right in front of Camden Hardware. I jumped into the phone booth and closed the door behind me just as appeal of thunder rocked the quiet little town.

It had been a million years since I had used a payphone, let alone called someone collect. Thank goodness there was a phone book in the booth with me. Thank goodness for unchanging small towns. I found the number I was looking for and went through the rigmarole of being connected. She answered on the first ring.

"Hello? What kind of telemarketer is this?"

I would've laughed if I hadn't been in such a hurry. "Sarahbeth it's Jason, please don't hang up! I really need to talk to you."

"No, I need to talk to YOU. I've been calling you all night! Why haven't you been answering? Where are you calling me from and why are you calling collect?"

"Take a breath! I went for a run and left my cell at the house."

"You went running in this weather?"

"It wasn't raining when I started out!"

"What number are you calling me from?"

"I'm on the payphone in front of Dad's shop."

"Why?" Sarahbeth didn't wait for me to answer. "It doesn't matter. I wanted to apologize. I had no reason to get jealous and I was being a total brat and I know it."

I tapped my foot against the phone booth floor and told myself to be patient. "Sarahbeth, it's ok. I was being vague and standoffish and you don't deserve that. You asked me a direct question and you were honest about your feelings and I was...I was noncommittal and that's not right. You're sweet and I do like you."

"I like you too, Jason."

"Ok good, cuz I need you right now... like, IMMEDIATELY!"

"Now that sounds more like it!"

"Not exactly like that, girl. Meet me at the payphone as soon as you can get here and Ill explain everything."

Sarahbeth sighed with feigned disappointment. "Fine."

"Oh and one last thing..."

"What is it your highness?"

"Can you bring me some dry clothes and a towel?"

Chapter Forty-Two

I STAYED IN MY PHONE BOOTH CAVE, OUT OF THE RAIN, UNTIL Sarahbeth pulled up in her little red car. I ran through the rain, opened the passenger door and got in. Sarahbeth squealed as I shook the rain from my hair. "Good gracious, you're soaked!"

"I told you!"

She threw a plastic bag on my lap. "There's a towel and some sweats in there."

I climbed into the backseat and as I changed I started to explain what I had heard at the diner.

Sarahbeth looked at me through the rearview mirror. "This is crazy! You think Ben and this other person know exactly what happened to Marc all those years ago?"

I had dressed in mere seconds and as I climbed back into the front seat I replied, "Yes. And Ben is going to lead us to whoever this other person is."

"What did you have in mind?"

"Simple, follow Ben from the café."

"When?"

"After they close so…", I checked my watch, "…shit they closed up five minutes ago!"

"Say no more!" Sarahbeth stepped on the gas and we hydroplaned a little as she did made a U-turn and headed back towards the café. We slid to halt half a block away and saw that Bojangles was dark. "Shit! Ben's car is gone!"

Sarahbeth was undeterred. "There's only a couple ways out of here. He couldn't have gone far. Let's just take a breath and start looking."

We went up one street and down another and within three minutes I saw taillights. "There!" I pointed to them as they made a right at the next block and Sarahbeth sped in their direction. We arrived at the corner, turned right and, sure enough, Ben's car was just ahead. We let Ben stay three car lengths ahead of us as we followed him.

It was dark even with the lightning and the rain was coming down strong. There weren't too many cars out and it was going to be hard to stay out of Ben's sight but what other choice did we have?

Sarahbeth couldn't shut up and she fired questions at me in rapid succession. "What is he doing? Do you think he saw us? Isn't he going to see us" What if I lose him?"

"Stop! Stop!" I pointed ahead. Ben had pulled over in front of a two-story home a block ahead.

Sarahbeth threw her hands in the air. "Brilliant, Sherlock. He's just going home." We watched as Shelly got out of the car and rant to the front door. Once she was inside Ben pulled the car away from the curb.

I patted Sarahbeth on the knee. "Nope. He was just dropping Shell off." Sarahbeth waited to a count of three before following Ben as he started back towards the restaurant. "Keep following him."

"I am!" Ben sped up and made the corner quickly.

"Stay with him!"

"Listen OFFICER, you want to drive?"

By the time we got to the corner Ben was gone. Sarahbeth sped up and slowed at each cross street while I looked right and she looked left.

I pounded the dash angrily. "Where did he go?"

"I don't know but could you not take it out on my car? It's not like he could just disappear."

I saw headlights about ten blocks ahead of us. Through the storm I could barely make them out but I was certain they were there. "There! Go get him!" Sarahbeth sped up.

"Not too fast or we are gonna wreck," I warned.

"Shut up! I know what I'm doing. I've been driving since I was fifteen!" Sarahbeth looked over at me clutching the dash. "Don't be such a baby! Geez, you're a cop. I thought you liked driving fast!"

"It's a different experience being a passenger. When your life is in the hands of a crazy redhead going Mach ten down a rain slicked road, you tend to get a little nervous."

Out of nowhere a swath of red and blue lights lit up the back window. Sarahbeth slowed as she looked in the rearview mirror. "Dammit!"

"Better pull over, kid."

"But we'll lose him!"

"It's not that big a town, kid. Ben isn't exactly going anywhere. I'll just have to find another way to get to him."

Sarahbeth pulled to the side of the road and waited for the officer.

I heard a tap on my window and rolled it down only to get pelted in the face with rain. A large beam of light shone right into my eyes.

"Well, who do we have here?"

"Hey Kirk."

Sarahbeth shouted at her brother, "Kirk! For god's sake its pouring. What the hell are you doing?"

"I was curious to see who was speeding along like a demon in this weather and now I'm glad I stopped you! You could have killed my sister!"

"What? Wait? I'm not the one driving!"

"Get out."

Sarahbeth yelled at Kirk again. "What? Kirk no!" To me she

whispered, "You don't have to put up with his crap. What's he going to do, shoot us?"

Kirk's voice became louder and he yanked open the passenger door. "I said, get out of the car, Camden!"

I peeled Sarahbeth's fingers from my sleeve. "It's fine. Just stay here." I stepped out of the car and for the second time tonight I was immediately soaked to the bone. I followed Kirk back to his car.

Kirk whirled around and stuck his finger in my face. "What the hell are you doing with my little sister?"

"Nothing. She picked me up because I had been out jogging when the storm hit."

"Stay away from her, Camden."

"Kirk, she's a grown adult and she can spend time with whomever she wishes."

Kirk grabbed me by the front of the shirt. I don't care if you're cop or the president of the united-fucking-states. You stay the hell away from my sister! I've been patient with you up until now because you're going back to that hellhole California in a few days. Frankly, Camden, that's the only reason. You want to keep poking your nose in where it don't belong? You go right ahead, but you leave my sister out of it."

I tried to pull away from Kirk but he pulled my face in closer. "I know everyone thinks your this great all American hometown boy turned city cop come home to visit and grace us with his presence but you want to know something? I think YOU had something to do with Marc's disappearance. I've always believed it and I always will."

"If I was the one responsible then why would I be investigating?"

"That's just it. I don't think you ARE investigating. I think you're finally trying to find someone to pin it on. Now that those papers in California have gotten ahold of the story you thought you better come home and clean up your mess. You thought you could salvage your reputation. Well guess what, I'm not going tot let that happen!"

Kirk let go of the front of my shirt and I stood there shocked at what he had said. I watched as Kirk stormed over to Sarahbeth's window. I could see them arguing for a few seconds before she slowly drove off down the street. Without. Me.

Kirk came back and as he was getting into his driver seat he pointed his finger at me over the windshield. "Stay away from my sister! And I want my sweatshirt back!" Kirk slammed his car door and drove off into the night with his overheads swirling in the dark. Without. Me.

I stood there in the middle of the street for half a second before turning and heading towards home. What a trip this was turning out to be.

I was soaked, my girlfriend's brother was out to kick my ass, I was being stalked and apparently the only sweatshirt Sarahbeth had been able to find belonged to Kirk.

I really missed California.

Chapter Forty-Three

I GOT HOME AND STRIPPED OUT OF MY WET CLOTHES. I THREW Kirks sweatshirt in the garbage. *Screw him!* I took a hot shower and went straight to bed. I was exhausted and even though my mind was a whirl of suspicion and anger, I easily fell into a dreamless sleep.

When I awoke in the morning there was no sign of last night storm. Everything was shiny and bright like nothing had happened. I lay there in my childhood bed for a moment going over the last night events.

Something Kirk had said struck me as odd. He said that California knew about Marc missing? I sat up quickly and reached for my phone. I pulled up the latest news and keyed in my name to see what would come up.

The first item to pop up was an article in Roland Confidential.

LOCAL COP; Third Shooting in Three Months

THE ARTICLE WENT on to give a lay by play of the three shootings I had been involved in during the course of my career. Tucked in among the "facts" and the insinuation that I was trigger-happy was one little, inflammatory sentence.

In 1991 Officer Camden was a person of interest in the missing person case of fourteen-year old Marc Forrester of Harmony Montana. The disappearance of Mark Forrester was never solved.

The byline was none other than my old pal Julie. I called her and she answered on the first ring.

"Julie, what the hell is the deal with this article?"

"Camden! I know, I'm sorry. I didn't write it. The new crime reporter did."

"Jules, the article has your byline. And do you mind telling me where your ace reporter got this information on my childhood friend?"

"You know we don't reveal sources, Jason."

"Blah, blah, blah. Save it, Jules! This is my life! This is my reputation!"

"He said he got a tip."

"What? A tip from who?"

"He said someone from your home town called him. That's all he would tell me."

"Julie, listen. This is not true and I'm going to prove it. You better jack that new reporter for not checking facts before printing that garbage or I'm going to sue his ass!"

"To be fair, weren't you a person of interest in that case?"

"I was fourteen and I had nothing to do with it!"

"Technically my reporter's facts are correct."

"Whose side are you on anyway? And what does it have to do with my shooting?"

"I'm on the side of the truth but I don't think you could possibly be involved. And yes, the article was skewed to be a little sensationalistic. I'll talk to him. And Jason, when you DO set the record straight you know who to call right?"

I slammed the phone shut. I liked Julie just fine. She had certainly been through her own share of drama where Roland P.D. cops were concerned but I was mad and I was holding this shit against her.

Chapter Forty-Four

I HAD TO THINK. THAT ARTICLE WAS GOING TO ADD MORE FUEL TO the fire in my most recent shooting investigation and I had to put a stop to it somehow.

I went to the kitchen to grab a cup of coffee and found both my parents had already left for work. I took my cup of coffee to the front porch and sat down on the porch swing. I stared out at the street where only a day before my car had been burned to the ground. This visit home had done the opposite of relaxing me. I was in pickle for sure.

I watched as the mailman made his way up the block, stopping at each mailbox and delivering bills, letters and packages to the occupants. Now that looked like a good job. No one to shoot, no one to confront, just stuffing envelopes into boxes and getting in some exercise to boot. I wondered if I could get a job like that when I was inevitably FIRED!

The mailman made his way up our walk and spotting me on the porch he cordially handed me the days mail.

I flipped through the stack of notices and junk mail and my heart stopped. There was an envelope addressed to Officer Camden. I turned it over in my hand. The envelope was your standard letter sized envelope with no distinctive markings. My name and address were hand written and I quickly realized there was no return address.

I slowly opened the envelope, a little nervous about what I may find.

I pulled out a single typed letter. My hands started to shake as I read it.

Stop looking for me. I don't want to be found.

NO WAY. This had to be a joke! This could not be from Marc, could it? What if he really had just run away and followed through with his fantasies of starting over? If he HAD done that, how did he know I was home and how did he know I was poking around? *The newspaper article.* If this not was really from Marc then why didn't he contact me in person or say more than these two cryptic sentences?

I checked the postmark and saw it had been stamped three days ago; before the article was released. The location said Deertail. *Ben.* He had gone to Deertail yesterday! Could he have sent this somehow?

I felt anger boil inside me. That same old anger that always seemed to seep through when my life got hectic. My adrenaline started pumping and I stood almost involuntarily, splashing my unfinished coffee onto Mom's front porch. No more playing around. I needed to stop this nonsense once and for all.

I WAS GOING to find out what happened to Marc once and for all and I knew just how I was going to do it.

Chapter Forty-Five

I SHOWERED AND DRESSED QUICKLY. I GRABBED MY PHONE AND walked the distance to the police department. I had a copy of Marc's missing person flyer and I was going to make a new one, with a few tweaks.

If I could get an age progression shot I could do a side by side and put it out. If, and this would be a big if, Marc was still alive someone somewhere would see it. IF Marc was still alive I needed to know and no note was going to dissuade me. If Marc were dead, this new flyer would be a notice to whoever was responsible that I was NOT giving up and I was more determined that ever to uncover the circumstances in question. I knew I could be taunting my stalker into performing an act more dangerous to my health than just vandalism but that was a good thing. I could deal more effectively with the stranger I could bring out into the open. Hopefully this flyer would do just that; bring someone out into the open.

I entered the police department and stepped up to the now manned receptionist window. A woman in her sixties sat behind the desk and a nameplate told me her name was Darlene.

Darlene looked up and smiled. I didn't recognize her but she seemed to know me. "Jason Camden! How can I help you? You need to make another police report? You get your car blown up this time?"

I didn't think her comments were all that funny. "No Darlene, I quit with the rental cars. I didn't want to be responsible for their inevitable bankruptcy due to loss of property."

Darlene laughed. "Well aren't you just a thoughtful young man. What can I do for you?"

"Is Kirk in?"

"No he's out on a call."

"What about the Chief?"

"The Chief in Billings for a conference for the next two days."

I was relieved but I made my face into an expression of disappointment. "Shoot. I really needed to talk to one of them." I leaned on the counter and gave Darlene my most innocent look. "Maybe you can help me? If I wanted to do an age progression on a photo of a kid could you do that?"

"You mean like you see on billboards?"

"Yeah, just like that."

"Sorry, we don't have that kind of computer program but you could call the FBI if it's regarding an open case. They have a Missing and Exploited Children Unit that does all that stuff." She opened her desk drawer and took out a business car. She wrote a number on the back. "Here, this is the number for the division you need."

I took the card even though I had no intention of using it. "Thank you, Darlene." I looked around the office behind her desk. "Is that a fax machine over there?"

"Sure is."

"I handed Darlene back the card she had given me. "Can you write down the number for me? I might need to have something faxed over from this FBI Unit you so graciously pointed me towards." Darlene took the card and as she wrote she asked, "You sticking around for the fair? There's gonna be a great dance and I might be convinced to save a dance for you?"

"I wasn't going to but I might have to now. What kind of man would I be if I turned down an invitation to dance with a pretty gal like you?"

Darlene winked at me as she handed me back the card with the fax number now written on it. "Say hi to your mom for me."

"I sure will!" I could feel Darlene's eyes watching me as I exited the building.

I know that involving the FBI would be tantamount to wrapping myself in red tape but I had another idea.

I took out my cell and dialed Lizzie.

"Jason! How's my favorite cowboy?"

"Awesome," I lied. "How's work?

"Same old thing different day but hey, I'm almost to a call. Can I call you back?"

"That's ok, I'll let you go but first, I have one quick favor to ask…"

"Shoot."

"I'm going to email you a picture. When you get a second can you run up to the Missing Person Unit and talk to someone about doing an age enhancement/age progression on it?"

"We can do that here?"

"We sure can." I added, "I'd call up there myself but I've currently got a love/hate relationship with the department and I'm afraid if I ask they wont give me what I need. I'm not supposed to be working as you well know."

"I get it. One question; just what am I supposed to tell them? No doubt the detective is going to ask me why I need this."

"I don't know. Flash those pretty eyes of yours, flip your blonde tresses and ask for a demonstration or something."

Lizzie snorted in mock derision. "Flirt my way to getting what YOU want, huh?"

"It's a mans world, lady. You're just playing it."

"Remind me to kick your ass for that when you get home."

"I'll see what I can do. Ok I've gotta go."

The last thing I heard before Lizzie disconnected was her sweet voice yelling, "Hey, you there! Stop!"

Never a dull moment.

I quickly emailed Lizzie the photo of Marc I had taken from the missing person poster and crossed my fingers she would be able to get me what I needed.

Chapter Forty-Six

IT WAS STILL EARLY AND I KNEW IT WOULD TAKE AWHILE FOR LIZZIE to get me what I needed. I decided I would run a few errands in the mean time. I stopped by the library and found Mom back amongst her treasured books.

"Hey Ma."

"Jason, What are you up to today?"

"I know you have a lot of baking to do before the carnival tomorrow. I just stopped by to see if you needed anything from the store? See if I could help out in any way?"

Ma's face lit up. "I sure do!" I watched as Ma went to a desk, grabbed a piece of paper and started furiously scribbling. "I have all the ingredients I need except for these few things." She handed me the paper. "Are you sure you don't mind? I will be off work in the next hour or so and then Ill be home to start baking."

"I would do anything for you, Ma. In fact, once you're finished here I will meet you at the house and we can work on those famous pies of your together."

Ma kissed my cheek. "What did I do to deserve such a good son?"

I shrugged, "You were just fortunate, I suppose."

Ma swatted me as I walked away. I exited the library and started towards the grocers. Two blocks later I paused at the open door of the Rec center. I could hear voices inside and one of them was Sarahbeth's. Last night had ended on a really weird note and I thought I had better check in on her.

I walked through the door and into the small office. For a minute I studied the paintings on the walls. Most of them appeared to have been painted by kids but I could see that some were adults and some were the work of Sarahbeth as well. Se really was talented.

I followed the smells of paint and turpentine down a short hallway and found the voice I was looking for. Sarahbeth was wearing a white smock that looked like Joseph's coat of many colors for all the paint that was on it. She had her head tilted to the side and she was looking at a canvas on an easel.

Next her sat a young boy, perched on a tall stool, paint brush in hand. Clearly she was in the middle of a session and I didn't want to interrupt. I found a chair against the wall and out of the line of sight and watched her work.

"Ok sweetheart can you tell me what you have here?"

The boy said, "It's a picture of my family."

"I see. And who are all these people?"

The boy pointed out each of the figures he had painted, "This is my mom and dad and me."

"Tell me about the colors you chose. Why did you painted yourself green?"

"Because I feel green."

"What does green feel like to you?"

I sneezed and they both looked up and spotted me.

"Sorry," I mouthed at her.

Sarahbeth smiled. She waved me over. "Come over here." I stood and walked to the easel. She tapped the boy in the head lightly. "I think you've met my nephew Mikey?"

Sure enough it was the thieving felon. "Hey man, how's it going?" I put out my fist and Mikey bumped it with his own.

He looked at me cautiously and then in true irritatingly honest kid fashion he said, "Aren't you that Jason guy who's a cop some-where else?"

I grimaced, "Yep. That would be me."

"My Uncle Kirk says you were the biggest scaredy-cat in town growing up."

Sarahbeth scolded him. "Mikey! Manners!"

I laughed. "Your Uncle Kirk was right. I was a scaredy-cat. What about you? Haven't you ever been scared of anything?"

Mikey squared his shoulders. "Nope. I'm not scared of anything!"

"Lucky you. I wish I had been that way at your age."

Mikey squinted at me with suspicion. "They let you be a cop if your scared?"

I shrugged. "I got over some of my fears but even as a cop I still get scared sometimes. And I bet your Uncle Kirk does too."

"Scared of what? I can't believe my Uncle Kirk is scared of anything. He's the bravest man I know."

I wanted to tell the kid that his "brave Uncle Kirk" was probably the biggest chicken in the world and that was why he was such a bully but I couldn't bear the thought of bursting his bubble. "Your probably right, kid."

Sarahbeth put an end to the conversation before it went some-where she didn't want it to go. "Ok Mikey, we are done for the day. I'll clean up and you go home and play."

"Thanks auntie."

As Mikey ran for the door Sarahbeth yelled out, "Go straight home!!"

"Yes ma'am," Mikey yelled back as he raced out into the sunlight.

I looked at the painting Mikey had done. "Well that was interest-ing. How's he doing?"

"Better. He's still a little shit but most of it is because he IS scared. He's holding on to a lot of anger and resentment over his dad's death and he doesn't even realize it." Sarahbeth slowly began collecting brushes and putting them into tin cans of paint thinner. "He idolizes Kirk but I wish he wouldn't." She paused and looked at me. "Don't get me wrong, Kirk is a great big brother and even if he is a little bit of a bully he makes a great cop for this town."

After last nights antics I could formulate a great argument for just why Kirk WASN'T a good cop for Harmony. "But?"

"But Kirk is a little too rule driven. Mikey needs more than just strict boundaries. He needs to understand where the anger comes from so he can let it loose once and for all. He needs to be able to vent it not reign it in."

I had tons of experience with folks who let their anger loose and it was never pretty. Sarahbeth was clearly an idealist but I was interested in her frame of reference. "Where do you think it comes from; this anger?"

"I believe he carries around guilt that he doesn't understand. When we lose someone we love, especially at such a young age, it can be extremely traumatizing. You of all people should know that."

I felt as if Sarahbeth had just slapped me. "What's that supposed to mean?"

"You lost Marc and you yourself told me that was when you stopped being afraid. I think that's when you started being angry and so you used that to fuel yourself into the job you have now. You drowned your fear with anger."

"I don't need my head shrunk."

"Are you sure about that? I know about the shootings you've been in and…"

I held up my hand to stop her. "You're checking up on me too?"

"Jason, all I'm saying is that your lack of serious romantic relationship, the fact that you put yourself in a high danger career and once there you keep putting yourself in the dangerous situations are all indicators of something deep inside you. Now your home for a visit and the first thing you do is start picking at an old wound. Drama junkie. Adrenaline junkie. Tell me the truth Jason. Do you have dreams as well? Nightmares?"

I looked at her with disdain and growing anger. "What the hell would you know about it? I'm not one of your kids, Sarahbeth. You're just a child yourself and have zero clue about what makes any man tick, let alone me." I turned away from her and stormed back the way I had come.

Sarahbeth was undeterred and yelled out after. "Come back! Jason, its understandable you wouldn't want to talk about it but you need to!"

I did what any grown, mature, self aware, man defending his honor would do; I held my hand up over my shoulder and flipped her off.

I was almost out on the sidewalk when I heard her yell, "Grow up!"

I STOMPED my way to the grocery store. Who did she think she was anyway? My girlfriend? Good lord that woman was frustrating. Prying one minute and throwing herself at me the next. I guess some would call that a modern woman but right now I'm so mad I just call it bullshit.

Man I can't wait to get the hell out of this place!

Chapter Forty-Seven

I REACHED THE GROCERY STORE AND QUICKLY FILLED MY MOMS shopping list. While I was waiting in line to pay, I heard my cell phone alert that a new message had through. I wasn't anxious to read whatever text Sarahbeth was sending my way but because I am a glutton for punishment I checked it anyway.

No text from Sarahbeth. An email from Lizzie. She had sent me the flyer I was waiting for! That girl was fast! A note accompanied the attachment. "You owe me!"

Oh girl, you have no idea how big I owe you!

I QUICKLY PAID for my groceries and hurriedly schlepped the bags towards home. Once there I unloaded the bags and put the items away.

I quickly changed into my running gear and jogged to the hardware store where I found Pop stocking shelves.

I was out of breath. Not from the jog over but from excitement. "Pop, I need to borrow your car for a few hours. Is that ok?"

"Where's yours?"

I cringed. "It had some mechanical issues so I returned it."

Pop fished his car keys from his jeans pocket. "Just make sure you're back in time to pick me up. I'll be closing up a little early so I can get home and help your mom get ready for the carnival tomorrow."

I quickly grabbed the keys from his hand. "You got it!" I ran out the door. I had to hurry if I was going to make it to Deertail and back in time.

Chapter Forty-Eight

I MADE IT TO DEERTAIL IN RECORD TIME AND FOUND MY WAY TO THE post office. Deertail was only slightly larger that Harmony but it was just as picturesque. I found a parking spot right outside the building and quickly went inside.

Luck was on my side. There was no line and I went straight to the front counter and dinged the bell for service. A twenty-something girl with purple hair and a nose ring met me at the counter.

"Can I help you?"

I took the envelope that had contained the note out of my pocket. "I received this in the mail yesterday and as you can see here it was postmarked from this office."

The wannabe punk rocker took the envelope and examined it. "Yup. Sure does." She smacked her gum and blew a bubble as she handed it back to me.

"I don't suppose there is anyway to tell WHO sent it?

The girl looked at me as if I was the one wearing black eyeliner and a purple mop on my head. "Nope."

I took out my phone and pulled up the flyer Lizzie had made me. "Can you take a look at this picture and tell me if you've seen this guy?" I shoved my phone as close to the girls face as she would let me.

"The kid or the old dude?"

"It's the same person," I explained. "Do you recognize the older version of the person in this picture?"

The girl shrugged. "I mean…he looks kinda familiar and all."

My heart leapt into my throat. "Seriously? You've seen this guy? In here?"

"Maybe. We get a lot of customers in here but I think I may have seen him once or twice."

"When was the last time you saw him?"

"Couple of days ago."

I stood in shock on my side of the counter and stared at the girl in front of me. She stared back. "Are you ok mister?"

My brain was spinning. "I'm fine." I pocket my cell phone and reached for the pain chained to the counter. I grabbed a mailing label from the stack next to the register and jotted down my cell number. "Here, please do me a favor. Call me the next time this guy comes in ok?"

The girl popped her gum once more. "Sure thing." She took the envelope and shoved it in her pocket.

I hurriedly left the post office and promptly realized I had left my keys on the counter. I re-entered the building and walked back to the counter. The girl was now on the phone, her back to the counter. "Yeah, you told me to call if that dude came in? Well he was here. Showed me some picture of a guy."

I stopped dead in my tracks. She was clearly talking about me. I prayed she wouldn't turn around and end her conversation.

"No…uh huh…sure. I told him I thought I recognized the guy in the picture just like you told me too. Yep…OK…" The counter girl still hadn't seen me. She walked through the side door and disappeared into the back somewhere, still talking on the phone.

I approached the counter but from my vantage point, I could no longer see the counter girl or hear her. I grabbed my keys and left without pursuing it further.

My anger was back.

Chapter Forty-Nine

I DROVE BACK TO HARMONY IN A FURY. WHAT THE HELL WAS GOING on here? I bet that girl had been talking to Ben. He and I were going to have to have it out at some point but there were a few things I needed to do first.

I made it back to the hardware store just in time to see Pop locking up. I met him at the door and handed him the key's. "Pop, thanks for the car. I'll meet you back at the house. I have a quick errand to run."

"Let me drive you."

"That's ok. Ma's probably waiting on you. I promise Ill be quick and home to help in an hour."

I set out on foot towards the one place I thought might hold an answer. It was a long shot but maybe something in Marc's old room would give me a clue to where he had gone, if he had in fact gone anywhere I could find him.

Chapter Fifty

I was pretty certain Mr. Forrester wasn't going to want to see my face but what other options did I have? I was willing to take the chance. I reached Marc's house in five minutes flat and nervously knocked on the door.

I waited to hear approaching footsteps but none came. I knocked again and waited. Nothing. I took a peak in the front window; the house is dark. I glance over at Marge Freelander's house but she is nowhere in sight.

I try the front door. Unlocked. I am definitely disregarding all common sense now. I open the door slowly and call out, "Mr. Forrester? Are you home?" I had no idea what I was looking for but I was going to look anyway.

I went to Marc's old room first but all these years later it appeared Mr. Forrester had been using it for storage. Old newspapers were piled everywhere amongst large trash bags of empty beer cans. Nothing of Marc's remained.

I closed the door and ventured further into the house. I found another door and opened it. Mr. Forrester's bedroom, in contrast to Marc's old room, was neat and tidy. I went to the dresser and immediately noticed a picture in a frame sitting on top. It was a picture of Marc as an infant, lying in the arms of a beautiful young woman. She must've been Marc's mother.

I opened the top dresser drawer and pushed aside socks and t-shirts. Underneath them I found a small photo album. I took it out and sat on the bed as I thumbed the pages. I flipped through pages filled with pictures of Mr. Forrester and his wife on their wedding day, happy portraits of a family I didn't even recognize and stopped short on a single photo of a beautiful portrait of Marc's mom. Marc was the spitting image of her, as much as a boy could be. I flipped to the next page and found a picture of Marc's dad smiling. Mr. Forrester looked so different back then. Aside from being so young his eyes were bright and his smile beamed from inside out. It made me sad to think of all that happened to turn this family inside out.

I continued to look through the pictures of depicting Marc as an infant, in the hospital with his mom. These must have been taken right after he was born. More pictures; a proud mom and dad bringing their infant home and a nursery decorated with baseballs and tractors.

I turned the page. No more pictures, just pages of newspaper clippings. An obituary for Marc's mom. Articles about Marc's disappearance. So much sadness.

I shut the photo album. I had seen more than enough. My heart softened towards Mr. Forrester. That man had been through too much pain.

I left the house as I had found it and made my way to the garage. The door creaked as I opened it and cobwebs hung in every corner. I pushed my way through them and made my way past fishing gear, a tractor and a rusty gun safe. Towards the back of the garage I found a large trunk. I pried the old clasp and found it contained Mr. Forrester's army memorabilia. I sifted through the moth eaten clothing and pushed aside the black and white snapshots that depicted a younger Mr. Forrester in his glory days.

And that's where I found it.

The army jacket Marc used to wear. The one and only real sign of affection his dad gave him. He had been wearing it he night we went to the quarry. I took the jacket out and held it up in the dim light. It had blood on it.

Chapter Fifty-One

I HEARD THE DOOR CREAK OPEN BEHIND ME AND I TURNED.

Mr. Forrester yelled at me, "What the hell are you doing I here?"

I was shaking. I held out the jacket. "Never mind what I'm doing here. What are you doing with this?" I yelled.

"My jacket?"

"Marc's jacket!"

Mr. Forrester raced towards toward me and grabbed at the jacket in my outstretched hand. "What are you talking about? That's MY jacket."

Mr. Forrester wrestled the jacket from my hand and I shoved him. He stumbled backwards.

I pointed an angry finger in his direction. My voice shook, "That is Marc's jacket. He was wearing it the night we went swimming, the night he went missing!"

Mr. Forrester's voice took on a softer tone and looked down at the article of clothing he held in his hands. "He was? Are you sure?"

"Yes, I'm sure! How the hell did you get it if he never came home that night?"

Mr. Forrester appeared confused now instead of angry. "I don't know. I mean, I found it on the front porch."

"It has blood on it." My voice involuntarily rose an octave. I felt like I was fourteen again. "You're a liar!" I demanded, "What did you do to him?"

Mr. Forrester looked at me with a puzzled expression. "Do to him? I didn't do anything to him. I loved my son more than anything."

"He was scared of you."

Mr. Forrester just stared at me with a vacant look in his eyes.

I continued my tirade and my words came out in stops and starts. "Marc was scared of you. He told me so. All your drinking. You didn't love him. You wished he was dead! You blamed him for his mother's death!"

"Is that what you really think?" His voice was so low I could barely hear him.

"It's what Marc believed."

Mr. Forrester burst into tears and I stood there stunned.

"Nothing could be further from the truth. I loved him so much. Marc was all I had left of my wife. I wasn't very good at showing it. What the hell did I know about raising a kid? But Jason, I would never hurt him." He looked at me with pleading, tear filed eyes and then lifted the jacket to his face and wiped them.

I found that I was suddenly starting to feel sorry for the man. "Ok, then where did the blood come from and how did it end up on your porch that night?"

"I have no idea. I saw it there in the morning, I told you. I was passed out drunk that night and in the morning I found this on the porch."

I pressed on. "Marge said she heard an argument that night. Could Marc have come home and fought with someone else without you hearing it?"

"I have no idea." Mr. Forrester looked ashamed. "When I drink, sometimes I black out and nothing can wake me."

I actually believed him. Was I getting soft? I reached my hand out, "Let me take the jacket in. I'll run it to the police and have the blood analyzed. It might be Marc's but it might not be. If someone hurt him the blood could tell us who. Would that be ok?"

Mr. Forrester reluctantly handed me the jacket without a word. I touched his shoulder. "I'm really sorry for everything you've lost and for all the years of misunderstanding you have had to deal with."

Mr. Forrester didn't respond and I pushed softly passed him and walked out into the night.

Chapter Fifty-Two

I WALKED SLOWLY HOME. I HAD A LOT OF THINKING TO DO AND I wanted to pull my thoughts and emotions together before facing my folks. When I reached the house I stood out on the sidewalk looking at the light in the window. I was dusk and I could see my mom and dad shuffling around the kitchen. The delicious smell of pie wafted through the open kitchen window and if I hadn't been holding a bloody jacket belonging to my childhood friend I would have said I was in the midst of a Norman Rockwell painting.

I opened the garage door and tucked the jacket behind a box on my one of my Dad's workbench shelves. Marc had been missing for fourteen years and while I was filled with an urgency to solve his disappearance, to find out how that blood had made its way to his jacket, to find out who was responsible for whatever had happened that night, I knew a few more hours wouldn't hurt.

I put a fake smile on my face, inside and well into the wee hours of the morning I worked alongside my folks as we got ready for the carnival the next day. Despite everything that had happened today, the time spent with them was soothing and when we finally cut the last light I was able to go to sleep immediately.

Chapter Fifty-Three

I AWOKE A FEW SHORT HOURS LATER, THE EARLY MORNING SUN streaming into my window and the smell of more pie wafting down the hallway. My Ma was a machine in the kitchen and by the time I was dressed and walking through the kitchen door, she was covered in flour and cherry juice.

I kissed Ma and poured myself a ht cup of black coffee. I looked around at the pies that covered every spare inch of counter space. "Ma, did you even sleep last night?"

"Of course I did. I got a few winks." She waved off the concerned look on my face. "I don't need much sleep these days, son. Besides, there were only a few pies left to make and I knew if I got an early start Id be able to rest easier this afternoon."

I shook my head. "What time do you need to be at the fair-grounds?"

"Not until six this evening. The carnival opens at eleven but I didn't feel like spending the whole day there. My pies will sell fast and I'll be able to enjoy the fireworks at dusk."

"I have an errand to run this morning but I'll be back in plenty of time to drive you and Pop to the carnival and help you get settled."

"That will be lovely, dear."

Chapter Fifty-Four

BY TEN I WAS DRESSED, APPROPRIATELY CAFFEINATED AND ON MY WAY
tot he police station with Marc's jacket safely wrapped in a brown
paper bag under my arm.

I really didn't want to take the chance of running into Kirk so I
called the Chief from my cell phone while I walked.

Once I had the Chief on the phone I asked to meet him in his
office and he agreed. When I reached the station, Kirk was standing
out front. He looked like he was on his way out so I loitered a half
block away until I saw him drive away.

Once Kirks patrol car was out of sight, I walked inside the
station and told Darlene I had an appointment with the Chief.
Within minutes she ushered me back to his office.

The Chief rose from his desk and shook my hand. "Jason,
you're phone call was a little cryptic but my interest is piqued. What
can I do for you?"

I relayed to the Chief the events of yesterday, including the
photo, the girl at the post office and my impromptu confrontation
with Mr. Forrester. I punctuated my story by laying the bag
containing Marc's jacket on his desk.

The Chief stared unflinching at the bag on his desk. "That's some story. Why call me and not Kirk?"

"I hate to say this but Kirk might be involved."

The Chief smirked. "Kirk might be a tool but I highly doubt he would do anything illegal as you suggest. We did a pretty thorough investigation fourteen years ago and we never found any evidence that Kirk was involved. If we had, we wouldn't have hired him."

I pushed the bag closer to the Chief. "Kirk may or may not be involved but he and I aren't exactly on speaking terms at the moment and this needs immediate attention."

"You think the blood on the jacket could be Marc's or possibly Marc's attacker...that is if he even was attacked. Did I get that right?"

"Yes. I just thought, if we could do DNA testing we could find another piece of the puzzle."

"You're a cop. You know as well as I do DNA testing doesn't happen overnight."

"I'm aware, but blood typing can happen sooner and you have Marc's blood type on file. If we type the blood and it doesn't match Marc's, we can reasonably assume the blood belongs to someone who knows something about Marc's disappearance."

The Chief nodded his head. "I'll take it and make sure it's handled immediately."

I got up from my chair. "Thank you, Chief. Just keep me in the loop. I know I don't have jurisdiction here but I sure as hell have an invested interest."

"Of course. You know, I'd love to have you on my force. You give any more thought to it?"

"Sure I've considered it but I'm not sure Harmony is the best fit for me. I'll make sure to let you know a soon as I decide."

Chapter Fifty-Five

I LEFT THE STATION JUST AS KIRK RETURNED. HE PARKED HIS PATROL car and jumped out to stop me. "What are you doing here, Camden? Haven't you caused enough trouble?"

I couldn't resist antagonizing Kirk a little. "The Chief was just offering me a job."

Kirks face flushed red but to his credit his voice remained neutral. "Are you going to take it?"

I verbally poked him further. "I just might. I've been giving it some serious consideration." The look on Kirk's face was priceless. I didn't wait for his response. I turned and walked away, gloating in the petty glory of yanking Kirk's proverbial chain.

Chapter Fifty-Six

I DROVE MY PARENTS TO THE FAIR GROUNDS AROUND SIX. IT WAS still bright out and the crowds were starting to form. I drove to the front entrance of the fairgrounds, let dad into the driver seat and mom and I started hauling out boxes of pies. We stacked them high in the rolling cart Ma had brought.

Dad drove off to park the car and I walked Ma to the booth to drop off her wares. We reached the booth assigned to baked goods and Ma went in ahead of me. I piled my arms with boxes of party and headed to the back of the booth. I could hear Marge an a couple other ladies talking and I paused because I could here Marge clear as day. I really had to stop with this eavesdropping thing.

I heard Marge say, "Are you happy having your son home for a visit?"

Mom replied, "Of course. We miss him terribly while he is away."

"Well he's sure been causing a stink."

"How do you mean?"

"Nosing around about that Marc kid. Dragging up old memories and running around accusing people of stuff they didn't do."

"Now Marge he's doing nothing of the sort." *That's right Ma, you*

tell her! "You know Jason and Marc were best friends. Asking questions is Jason's way of putting old ghosts to rest and who are we to
say his way of healing is wrong?"

Marge apparently couldn't be dissuaded and the fact she had an
audience seemed to egg her on. "If I remember correctly he was
questioned in that case, wasn't he?"

Ma was unfazed. "Yes, Marge, he was."

"Well I feel sorry for you, Susan. I really do."

"Sorry for me? Why? Jason is innocent."

"How would you know? He snuck out without you knowing a
thing about it, didn't he? Went all the way down to the quarry with
Marc and then came home without him. I bet if we drag the lake
we will find the body of that poor Marc."

"They already did that, Marge and it wasn't found."

Man my Ma was tough.

Marge pressed Mom harder. "Well maybe your just helping him
cover it up? Who wants the whole town to know their own kid is a
murdering psychopath? It's in his nature. I've read all those articles
in the paper. Your son has made quite a career of shooting people!"

Before I could storm in and punch Marge straight in her big fat
nose, a man's voice sternly interrupted. "Marge Freelander!
Enough!"

"Jason was a good friend to my Marc and I have full confidence
he had nothing to do with it. Your gossiping and accusations are
doing no one any good and you'd be doing everyone a huge favor if
you just the hell up." *Go on with your bad self, Mr. Forrester!*

I entered the booth, set down my armful of boxes and glared, as
everyone looked my way. I stared at Marge, willing her to say just
one more thing. Marge looked away, stubborn and unrepentant.

Mom put her hand on my chest and pushed me back towards
the exit. "Come on son, let's get the rest of the stuff". Mr. Forrester
came alongside my mom and took her by the arm. We all walked
towards a near by picnic table and Mr. Forrester helped Ma take a
seat.

"Don't you worry about that gossip monger, kid." He turned to
Ma. "Susan, I'm really sorry about what that woman said to you."

"Now John, you know we are all family here and I appreciate you sticking up for me but it was unnecessary. Marge is just an unhappy old woman."

I marveled at my mother strength. "Ma you never have a bad word to say against anyone, do you."

"It's the Christian thing to do, to be kind and turn the other cheek."

Mr. Forrester and Ma continue talking but something, or rather someone has caught my eye and the world around me has gone silent.

He's been watching us and while I can't see him especially clearly I can see he sees me watching. He notices me looking back and turns and pushes into the crowd.

No way. It can't be. He looked JUST like the picture Lizzie had sent me. He looked just like Marc.

I got up quickly. "Mom will you be ok if I leave you for a moment?"

Mr. Forrester said, "I'll keep her company until your dad gets here."

"I'll be just fine son. You go on ahead."

I give her a quick peck on the cheek and head into the growing crowd.

Chapter Fifty-Seven

The Marc look-a-like was walking fast and if I didn't know better I would think he was trying to avoid being seen. I saw him cast a few glances around before racing up the entrance to the funhouse.

I FOLLOWED SUIT.

I PUSHED past three little kids. Threw a ticket at the carney holding the curtain and went in. *God I hated these things.* I craned my neck to see ahead of the people blocking my way and caught a glimpse of my target up ahead. If this person really was Marc, why would he be avoiding me? Why was he hiding? He had been watching me, and his dad. Has he known I've been looking for him?

I lose sight of the man at the next turn and as I make the corner a clown pops up. I'm not going to lie. I almost punched it. I hated clowns.

I make my way through the whole funhouse but when I come out the other side, the man is gone.

Was I losing it? The phrase Mental Breakdown comes to mind.

I make my way to the nearest beer tent, buy a frosty beer and guzzle it. I take out my phone and call Lizzie. I needed to hear her voice.

She answers but all I can eek out is, "HI, its me."

"What's wrong? She can hear the strain in my voice.

"Nothing, its just, I …I want to come home."

"Why? What happened?"

"Ill deny it if you ever repeat it but I think I'm seeing things! Maybe finally having that mental break down everyone warns you about when you start the force."

"Well it's no wonder. You've been through a lot. You tend to stay so busy you don't give yourself the time you need to fully process it all."

"You think?"

"I know! You're a man and men don't like to open up. I get that, but Jason, if you come home now, without dealing with all that's going on, nothing will change."

"You want to change me, huh? Ain't that just like a woman?"

She laughed. "That's not what I'm saying. Nice try at changing the subject though."

I got serious again. "You know how it is, Lizzie. Anyone at work starts to have a problem and they put you in the nuthouse. The guys don't get it."

"I think more men would understand if more men would talk about what they are going through. You HAVE to know you aren't the only one, right?"

"It's the culture, Lizzie."

"Well if you won't talk to a professional you always have me. But I'm probably just as screwed up as you are."

The thought of Lizzie suffering made my heart hurt. "I'll always be here for you, kid."

"I know."

I cleared my throat. "When I get home…. I'd like to spend some time with you."

Silence stretched between us as I waited for her to say something. Had I just blown it?

"I think I'd like that too. But don't come home like this, Jason. Do what you went there to do."

"I came home to relax but all that's happened is that I've gotten all worked up."

"That's not the only reason you went home. I think you knew somewhere inside that the root of your problems were in Montana and you went home to dig them out."

"How do you know me so well?"

"I'm a woman. Women know these things."

"You're the best partner I've ever had."

"And don't you forget it!"

"Thanks for answering when I call."

"Talk soon ok?"

I HANG DISCONNECT. The cool evening air, the buzz obtained by beer and my conversation with Lizzie has taken takes the edge off and I'm starting to feel like normal again.

I make my way back to the center of carnival and run right into Sarahbeth, Ben and Shelly.

Crap. There goes my blood pressure.

Chapter Fifty-Eight

SARAHBETH TOOK MY ARM. "ARE YOU OK?"

Ben looked at me warily. We hadn't spoken since the night at Bojangles. "Hey man, this party is cookin!"

Shelly smiled sweetly. "Hi sweet thang. You wanna join u?. We are headed to the Ferris wheel."

I nodded and Sarahbeth put her arm through mine as if she hadn't left me standing in the rain only days earlier. We walk to the ride in silence and once Sarahbeth and I are settled in the rides swaying car, she rest her head on my shoulder. As we go round and round she snuggles in close. On our fifth time around, the ride stops. Our car is stopped at the highest point and it sways gently in the night air. I look over the edge. "What's happening?"

Sarahbeth squeezes my arm. "Ssh. Just watch." Music starts to play and I hear the national anthem. When the music stops fireworks light up the night sky. We have the best seat in the house.

"Wow, this really is something."

Sarahbeth smiles, "There really is no place like home is there?"

Chapter Fifty-Nine

AFTER THE RIDE IS OVER AND WE HAVE DISEMBARKED I EXCUSE myself to go find my folks. Sarahbeth doesn't even try to hide her disappointment but I'm really not in the mood to deal with her. I am halfway to the parking lot when a hand grabs my arm. I spin around and find Shelly, alone.

"I need to talk to you."

"Not tonight Shell, I'm beat and I have a lot to do tomorrow."

"I heard you found Marc's jacket."

This got my attention and my exhaustion was replaced with a tingle of anxiety. "How did you know about that?"

"Kirk."

"Figures."

"Can we go for a ride? I think we need to talk."

"You're forgetting, I don't have a car."

"I drove. I sent Ben to the store and told him I'd meet him there."

I agree to the ride and Shelly and I find her car parked in the lot. Shelly starts the car and we drive in silence as we leave the fairgrounds. Once we are on the main road back into town Shelly starts to talk. "Look, Jason, you have to understand. We were just kids back then."

"Shell, what are you talking about?"

"I need to show you something." Shelly drove through Harmony and then five miles to the west. She turned onto a dark gravel road that led to Old Man Frasier's farm and she stopped. She cut the headlights and turned to me in the dark. "It was me."

"Huh?" My brain wasn't registering anything other than the darkness.

"I killed Marc."

Chapter Sixty

I tried to get my eyes to focus in the dark interior of the car. I felt an overwhelming need to see Shelly's face. "Shelly, what are you talking about?"

"It was an accident. There was a party that night and we had all been drinking…"

"I know about the party but Ben said you weren't there."

"He was just trying to protect me. But this has gone too far."

I couldn't speak. I couldn't think. I wasn't registering what Shelly was saying.

"The night you and Marc went to the quarry, we had a huge party at the Thompson house. Someone called the cops and we all ran. Ben and the guys, they all got caught but I hid in yard under some stinky old tarp until the cops had gone."

My voice was cold as ice, "What did you do."

Shelly took a deep breath and her voice shook. "I waited until the cops were gone and then I got in Ben's truck and started to drive home. I wasn't even going very fast but I must've been drunker than I thought. I was almost to the edge of town when I hit something."

"Something?"

"Someone." Her words spilled out in a torrent that matched the rushing noise in my ears. "I didn't even see him. He just came out of nowhere and I heard a thud and when I went to check what the noise was I found him. I must've hit him hard because his bike was off to the side and he was bleeding so badly. I've never been so scared in my entire life!"

I fought back the vomit threatening to rise. "Shelly, where is he?"

"I left him there and raced to the police station. I was going to tell, I swear I was. I was sure I could get help but when I got there Ben was walking out the front door and found me hysterical on the front steps."

"He was already out of jail?"

"You know how it was back then. They didn't want to waste their time on a couple kids drinking and Ben was the soberest of them all. I guess they thought it was easier to send him than keep him for the night."

"What happened next?"

"I told Ben what happened and he told me not to say anything. Jason, he wouldn't let me tell! Instead, Ben drove us back to the spot I had hit Marc."

"You didn't get any help?"

"It wouldn't have mattered, Jason. Marc was dead by the time we got back."

I was horrified. I got out of the car and stood on the side of the dirt road, holding back a scream.

Shelly got out of the car and came around to me. She grabbed my arm in desperation. "I would do anything to go back and change what happened but I can't. I was just a kid and Ben said that I would go away fro murder if anyone found out what had happened."

I pushed Shelly away from me. "Where is he Shell. Where is Marc's body."

Shelly pointed out into the darkness of the trees that surrounded us. "He's over there. Ben and I brought his body here and buried it." I grabbed Shelly's arm as hard as I could. "Show me. Show me exactly where!"

"It's too dark. You wont be able to see anything. Jason please, let go of me!"

I shoved her away again. "Get in the car."

Chapter Sixty-One

I put Shelly in the passenger seat, got into the driver seat and started the car. I turned to her, "Why now? Why tell me all this now?"

"You've been badgering everyone about Marc's disappearance and we've all been scrambling to keep it hidden. I just can't take it anymore. It's eating me alive!"

As it should! You killed someone! Not only that, you let me, Marc's dad, everyone in town wonder what the hell could've happened to him!" I put the car in drive. I was so disgusted I couldn't think straight. I made a U-turn on the dirt road, the tires spitting gravel into the air.

"I did leave a note."

"You did what?"

"That night. After Ben dropped me off back at home. I couldn't sleep. I was so scared. Somehow Marc's jacket got left in the back-seat of my car so I snuck over to his house and left it on the porch."

"With a NOTE?"

"I pretended it was from Marc and I wrote that he had left town, runaway. He was always talking about leaving this place. I figured his dad wouldn't hurt so much if he thought Marc had just up and left."

"No one found a note Shelly."

"I know. I have no idea what happened to the note but I swear I left it there." Shelly paused as we entered town. "Where are we going?"

"Where do you think? To the police station! You are going to tell Kirk everything you know!"

"NO! I can't do that! We will lose everything! Jason, please, we were just kids."

"You, you and Ben both, should be in jail for the rest of your lives."

Shelly's voice changed from pleading to utter coldness. "You can't prove anything."

"Prove? That's what your worried about? How about the fact you drove me out to where Marc's body is?"

"You could just as easily have done it yourself, buried Marc. Everyone knew you were the last person to see him alive."

I ignored Shelly and drove straight to the police station. She was right. It was going to be her word against mine but I didn't care. I went around to Shelly's side of the car and yanked open the door. I grabbed her by the arm and pulled her with me towards the front of the police station. She didn't make a sound.

I open the door and pull Shelly inside. I yell out, "Hello? Anyone here?"

Kirk poked his head out from the back room and seeing me gripping Shelly by the arm he quickly walks to the lobby. "What in the hell are you doing Camden? Let go of her!" Kirk pulls my hand from Shelly's arm.

"She's under arrest, Kirk.!"

"What the hell for?"

"She killed Marc!"

"Ok Camden, I've had just about enough of your crap."

Shelly spoke up, "It's true, Kirk."

"Kirk looked at her with a concerned look, "Shelly?"

"I'll tell you everything but first, can you call Ben?"

Chapter Sixty-Two

IT WAS WELL AFTER THREE IN THE MORNING WHEN I FINALLY GOT home and snuck to my room. I didn't even bother to undress. I lay on my bed, in the dark and let the tears fall freely. I had stayed at the station and joined Kirk in the interview room while Shelly and Ben poured out all the details of that horrible night.

Ben had admitted that he was the one who had been trying to scare me off of the investigation. He thought that by smashing my car, burning the other car and sending me on a wild goose chase with the note from "Marc" he could frustrate me enough that I would leave.

Shelly cried her little eyes out but I felt no sympathy for her. What she and Ben had done, and then covered up was the worst tragedy of my life; of Mr. Forrester's life.

I wasn't sure how I was going to get through what came next.

Chapter Sixty-Three

It had been a week since Shelly's confession. With her and Ben's help, Kirk and the Chief had located Marc's body. His bike had been buried right along with him.

Marc's dad had arranged a second funeral and this time, I was there. The whole town had come out to pay their respects. I had stood by the graveside watching everyone around me mourn for a second time.

Kirk in his class A uniform. Mikey clinging to Sarahbeth's hand, her red hair blowing in the wind like the day I met her. She had stared at me with sad wide. Marc's dad looked better than I'd ever seen him; sober. And Mom and Dad were right by his side.

Marc's dad gave a eulogy. He talked about how much he loved Marc and how he was finally at peace.

Peace. I too felt a little more at peace. Shelly and Ben had been taken over to he county seat and booked into the county jail. The D.A. was still trying to decide what charges, if any, he would bring against them.

I had telephoned Lizzie and told her everything. She had been so comforting and strong.

My captain had called yesterday and advised me I was clear to return to duty. I had immediately made arrangements to fly back as soon as possible.

Harmony would always be my home but I had a future waiting for me out in California. I knew that future it would be waiting for me the minute I stepped of the airplane and into her arms.

www.ingramcontent.com/pod-product-compliance
Lightning Source LLC
Chambersburg PA
CBHW061214170626
46809CB00003B/1346